TWO PRINCES OF SUMMER

NISSA LEDER

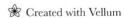

www.nissaleder.com
facebook.com/nissa.leder
twitter.com/nissaleder

Chapter One

❦

G raves had always freaked Scarlett out. Dead bodies trapped in boxes for all eternity and buried six feet under the ground. No. Thank. You. If Scarlett had any choice, she would be far away from the garden of the dead. But her mom now rested there in a cherry wood casket. It was mostly her sister Ashleigh's decision, but when Ashleigh asked Scarlett if she liked it, Scarlett nodded. How could she possibly *like* something that would hold her mother's dead body for the rest of eternity? But the red hue of the wood reminded Scarlett of her mother's hair, so as far as caskets went, it worked.

The sun hid behind the gray clouds as Scarlett neared the edge of the hill overlooking the cemetery below. Everything was still. Not even a bird chirped. Aside from Scarlett and her sister, the cemetery was void of people, at least anyone *living*. Many of the headstones scattered about had bouquets on them—some new, some withered. Others were bare.

Scarlett should keep walking. One foot in front of the other. Simple, usually. But her legs felt like cement blocks as she peered down at the sea of graves. Ashleigh was already halfway down the slope without even a look back. She walked straight to their mom as she always did.

Scarlett plopped crisscross on the ground as she watched Ashleigh like some stalker too afraid to get near. The ground chilled Scarlett's bare legs, but she didn't mind.

So much for acting like an adult. Scarlett turned eighteen one month before her mom's death. They'd celebrated together by buying a hundred bucks worth of scratch tickets—only fifteen dollars of which they recouped—while filling their stomachs on pizza and candy. Her mom seemed normal that day.

Scarlett had made it through childhood seemingly unscathed. Sure, her life was complicated at times, but that moment, as she morphed from kid to adult with the one person she loved most, was perfect. Optimism swam through Scarlett, but her high didn't last long. And the fall crushed her from the inside out.

She rolled the flower stem in her hand. A petal fell to the ground between her legs. Great. She ruined it. Now if she found the courage to keep going, she'd have nothing to leave. Then again, it had been six months since they buried her mom and she still hadn't found the strength to visit. She doubted today would be any different.

Scarlett had always wished for more from life. More

excitement. More surprises. More something. She craved new adventure. So much so, she never appreciated what she had. Now her mom was gone, and, despite her mom's fits and outbursts, all Scarlett wanted was to have her back.

The cool breeze from the storm rolling into town caused goosebumps to rise on Scarlett's skin. She inhaled the spicy smell of the Evergreen trees around her. So much death in one place was depressing. A sadness lingered in the air where loved ones grieved the ones they'd lost.

Scarlett had spent so much of her life embarrassed by her mother, which, to some, was just a normal part of life. But unlike her friends who wished their mothers wore different clothes or drove different cars, Scarlett's mother spoke to people who weren't there. Hallucinations plagued her. And, though Scarlett seemed normal to everyone else, she sometimes wondered if she, too, was *different* somehow.

An insecure teenage girl, shocker. It wasn't her hair or her clothes that made her feel out of place, though. Something else sent an *off* feeling through Scarlett. Something she couldn't quite put a finger on.

She fit in well enough with her classmates. She was liked by most, guys especially. The attention from them made her buzz inside. Sometimes too much. The more they wanted her, the more energized she felt, as if she could absorb the lust radiating from them. A shrink would probably say she had daddy issues or something. Well, lack-of-daddy issues, since she'd never met her father and knew absolutely nothing about him.

Now she didn't even have a mother.

With only silence to listen to, she lost herself in memories: her mother's body sprawled on the ground with limbs in unnatural positions, blood pooled at her sides. Nausea hit Scarlett. She tried to think of anything else, but the memory consumed her as it had so many times. As hard as she tried, she couldn't forget the image.

Her mother's upturned wrists revealed a vertical slit on each arm.

Suicide.

❧

AN AURA OF SORROW, anger, and guilt always surrounded graveyards: an emotional feast for Cade. He had spent the weekend practicing his battle skills and now his magic ran low. His mother discouraged him leaving Faerie, the fae realm, so often—he wasn't as protected outside the Summer Court—but Cade found human emotion the most fulfilling. Most humans in his realm were servants who had exchanged their freedom for the kind of release only the fae could offer, their emotions already numbed by someone else. So, from time to time, Cade came to the mortal world to find untouched rage, sorrow, elation, and any other strong feelings to refuel.

A young woman sat along one of the newer graves, her strawberry blonde curls swaying in the breeze. The wind carried the warm scent of her freshly shampooed hair. He'd seen her before, always placing a single rose onto the earth. He'd fed from her emotion, but it didn't satisfy him. She had sadness, sure, but nothing more than a small first course. Likely one of those optimistic types who saw the good in everything, even death. What good there was in dying, Cade didn't know. The fae could die, but they didn't suffer from disease or old age as often or as soon as humans did.

Usually there were others visiting the buried bodies, but today there was no one else. Perhaps the dark gray clouds rolling into town scared the humans away. Cade didn't understand why humans spent so much of their time and their feelings on the dead. But grief was a strong emotion and an easy source of replenishment.

The girl gently set a yellow rose down on the ground in front of the headstone. Cade was about to give up and try a bar instead. Alcohol stimulated emotion and people could be found there even in the middle of the day, drinking away their problems, as if puking somehow purged their sorrows. As he scanned the graveyard one last time, he noticed movement on top of the hill above. Another young woman sat there. She peered down the hill, still. Within a blink of the eye, Cade evanesced himself to the girl. Even though he wore his invisible glamour, he kept his distance and hid behind a tree, its branches grazing his skin.

This girl shared a resemblance to the other. Both had light blue eyes and freckles sprinkled across their noses, but this girl's hair was a dark brown, the opposite of the light tone of the other. And unlike the other girl, a surge of emotion surrounded her. Cade inhaled slowly, allowing his aura to absorb her feelings. Sadness, fear, and guilt mixed. This girl was avoiding something.

Cade had never tasted such intense turmoil.

IT HIT HER QUICKLY— the hole in her soul. Like a chipped windshield, once cracked, the pain spread and flooded Scarlett. She looked down and, in the distance, saw Ashleigh lay down today's rose. She should be there, too, but she was weak. How was she supposed to move on if she couldn't even visit her mom's grave? The pain swelled inside her until she was ready to burst.

Something else hit her. A presence of some sort, as if she were being watched. The emptiness inside her felt almost plugged. Suddenly, she didn't feel so sad. So broken. Scarlett glanced around. She saw no one else in the opening of trees where she waited. If she believed in ghosts, she might have thought her mother had visited her. But she didn't. She didn't know what to believe anymore.

Ashleigh thought their mother had escaped her worldly pain and now spent her days on streets of gold. Scarlett wanted to believe her mother had finally found her paradise. No matter where her mother resided now, Scarlett had to believe she wasn't in pain. Wherever where she was, she was gone. Scarlett couldn't ask her for advice, couldn't laugh with her until they cried. Her mom wouldn't be there to watch her walk down the aisle. She couldn't hold Scarlett's future children. It was unfair and stupid, and, most of all, it just plain sucked.

As the pain crept back in, the pressure in her chest flared. Before she burst into tears as she had every day since her mother died, a calmness rushed through her. Nothingness replaced the knife that pierced her heart.

Something was wrong. The grief Scarlett should feel had vanished.

She was numb.

Chapter Two

S carlett was five when everything changed. She and Ashleigh were playing with dolls in Scarlett's room when they heard their mom scream. Ashleigh hid under the bed. Scarlett, the brave soul she was, rushed to the living room.

Her mom shouted at someone to leave her alone. She gripped her ears, eyes clamped shut. No one else was there. Fear coursed through Scarlett. Would her mom be okay? What if she wasn't? The panic swam through Scarlett's veins like a raft down furious rapids, destined to crash. Her mind repressed the next few hours, gone from her memory like a ship lost at sea. Eventually, Scarlett's mom calmed down and told the girls not to worry. It was just a freak incident. Things were fine.

But the voices kept coming, and Scarlett would often hear her mom talking to someone who wasn't there. Her once vibrant and happy mom turned lethargic and apathetic. That was when Scarlett's love for the piano began. She'd sit at its bench for hours at a time, pressing down the keys randomly as she made up her own songs. It didn't matter how it sounded as long as it blocked out the noise of her mother talking to nothing and kept Scarlett from worrying about what would happen if the voices didn't stop.

When Scarlett's grandma came to visit, she noticed the change in her daughter, and, after a weekend of begging, Scarlett's mom agreed to see a doctor.

Schizophrenia—the doctor said—which, with medication, could be managed. And, at first, things got better. Until Scarlett's mom said the pills made her feel funny and she didn't need them.

The cycle continued over and over—on the pills, off the pills—until Scarlett accepted her life for what it was.

SCARLETT AND ASHLEIGH walked home silently. The cemetery was about a mile from their house—both convenient and creepy. Rain drizzled as they turned into their neighborhood, coating everything with a fine layer of dampness. Scarlett might have been worried about its effect on her hair if she cared about things like that anymore.

Right after their mom had died, the sisters hugged each other and cried. Scarlett had never felt as close to Ashleigh as she had in that moment. Maybe it would be their chance to be loving sisters, Scarlett had thought. The kind who believed each other when no one else did. She wanted a sister who had her back. Any hopes Scarlett harbored had disappeared after the funeral. Since then, Ashleigh barely spoke to her. They ate their meals together with nothing more than "pass the salt" from Ashleigh's lips. Not even a "please."

"What did I do?" Scarlett blurted as they stepped onto their porch, its old wood creaking beneath their feet.

"Huh?" Ashleigh asked, taking her hand off the doorknob.

"You barely even look at me anymore."

Ashleigh rolled down the sleeves of her yellow cardigan. "It's just hard, okay?"

"What's hard?" Scarlett stood with her arms dangling at her sides.

"Losing mom."

"It's hard for me, too, Ash."

"I'm sure it is." Ashleigh rolled her eyes as obviously as possible.

"What's that supposed to mean?"

"You always complained about how hard your life was. I'm surprised you're not happy she's dead."

The words pierced her heart. Scarlett knew her attitude had sucked. Didn't Ashleigh know how horrible Scarlett felt? She wasn't a genie, though. She couldn't take it all back. And life with her mom was hard—the paranoia, the compulsion, the apathy.

Of course, Ashleigh would judge Scarlett. Flawless Ashleigh who never broke curfew. Who never got a bad grade. Who always wore a smile on her face no matter what kind of day their mom was having. She didn't worry that she'd inherited their mom's illness.

Ashleigh was good without trying—an angel sent from the heavens. Scarlett might have been a devil, but at least she was one who desperately tried to grow wings. She just sucked at it.

"I know I messed up a lot. I'm trying to be better," Scarlett said.

"It's too late, Scarlett. Mom *died*."

Scarlett clenched her teeth. The breath froze in her lungs. Ashleigh's words cut through flesh and dug into Scarlett's soul, a million needles twisted into her heart. She screwed up sometimes. Maybe it *was* her fault. It didn't matter anymore, though. Their mom was gone. Nothing could bring her back.

Without another word, Scarlett stomped past Ashleigh and went straight to her mother's room, slamming the door behind her. The sweet smell of her mother's perfume still lingered. Scarlett crawled into bed and under the covers like she did as a child. It had always been her safe place—from the boogie man to a bad day at school, the one place she could go and everything would feel okay again. It wasn't the same without her mom there, but it still comforted her. She barely slept at night anymore. When she dozed off, nightmares tormented her until she woke screaming. Were they the first step in losing her mind? First, nightmares. Next, voices? She wondered what her mom's first symptom was. Lack of sleep drained Scarlett, and, right then, all she wanted to do was fall asleep and forget her life.

THE SUN WARMED Scarlett's face, seeping into her fair skin as her back pressed into the cold ground below. She peered into the perfectly blue sky and searched for shapes in the cumulous clouds. Something was different. How did she get here? The last thing she remembered was falling asleep in her mother's bed.

She must have been dreaming.

Her mind relaxed as she waited in the middle of an open meadow. Red, blue, and yellow flowers were scattered amongst the tall green grass. Calmness had become a foreign feeling to Scarlett. She welcomed the serenity it held. A gentle breeze blew her dark locks. This wasn't real. It couldn't be. She'd never been to this meadow before. But it didn't feel fake either. It was unlike any dream she'd ever had.

"Hello," a voice said behind her. It didn't startle her. It was as if she'd expected it to come. With a tone warm like honey, she relaxed even more. Her weight sank into the earth as tranquility washed over her.

Scarlett pushed her body to a sitting position and turned to see a young man nearing. He approached her with an extended hand. She'd read somewhere that everyone in their dreams was someone they'd seen before, but she was certain if she'd seen this face, she'd have remembered. His eyes were aqua, and Scarlett felt lost in them as if they were as vast as the Caribbean Sea. She reached instinctively for his hand, which burned hotter than her own.

"You're beautiful," he said.

He was beautiful, not her. The two sides of his face

aligned in perfect symmetry, with ears pointed ever-so-slightly, Scarlett almost didn't notice. His skin was smooth as silk, but his aura burned hot. Scarlett's awe kept her silent. Who was he?

He locked his fingers with hers. His piercing eyes stirred her stomach.

"Who are you?" Scarlett asked.

His mouth curved into a half smile. "Cade," he said, "but more importantly, who are *you*?"

"Scarlett."

He leaned into her and inhaled the scent of her neck.

Scarlett's eyes closed as her nerves prickled. She wanted to press her body into his. She needed to. Scarlett had never felt such desire before. Nearly unnatural desire.

Cade wrapped his free hand around her and pulled her toward him.

Why was she acting like this? She didn't even know him. Sure, Scarlett had done her share of things with guys. But she'd never felt so out of control of herself. His mouth nibbled on her neck. A sigh escaped her lips. Her body fell further into his and her hands moved to his chest.

Cade's mouth grew more aggressive on Scarlett's neck until he groaned.

The air around Scarlett cooled as Cade's touch left her.

"Sorry, beautiful. Duty calls." He let go of her hand and stepped backward. "Don't worry. I'll find you again." After the words left his mouth, he disappeared.

Scarlett jolted upright in her bed.

"OF COURSE you'd ruin my perfectly good dream," Cade said as he pulled out of Scarlett's mind. Raith's voice had broken his connection to her.

Scarlett. Such a lovely human. Something about her called to Cade. To be so infatuated with a mortal wasn't something he'd admit to. But after only a few minutes of her in his dreamscape, magic blazed again through his veins. His training had grown brutal over the last two weeks. His mother insisted he intensely prepare himself for the upcoming battle against his brother. Cade didn't see Raith as much of a threat. As far as he knew, Raith didn't even train. But Raith was older, his mother constantly reminded him, and had had more time to learn his power.

"To live in dreams is a waste of reality, dear brother," Raith said. "Preying on the innocent little humans."

Raith's loose tan shirt was half untucked from his pants as if he'd just rolled out of bed. Sloppy, if you asked Cade. That and his unruly chin length hair made him look more like a beggar than a prince.

"Oh, please. I give them good dreams that they won't even remember." Cade pushed himself up from his bed. "What do you care? You don't even associate with them."

Raith shrugged. "The king wants to see us."

Cade followed Raith to the battle wing of the castle. Here, the new military recruits trained each spring. The Summer Court hadn't been attacked in years. They'd defeated the Winter Court a half-century ago in a small war, but still, the threat of another attack kept young, sturdy Summer fae signing up to keep the kingdom strong. Cade was too young to know anything but the history of the war. Now that summer had come, this part of the castle was empty except for Cade and Raith's training. At the end of the summer, Cade would challenge Raith for the Right of Heir. As the oldest son of the King, Raith was granted the title until Cade, his only sibling, was of age. Any time after age nineteen, a younger sibling could battle against the current heir. Most waited years, as fae power was unpredictable and harder to manage in early adulthood. But their father grew weaker every day, and Cade's mother urged him to challenge right away.

The temperature of the battle wing was at least ten degrees cooler than the other parts of the castle. Cold suppressed his power but promoted magic alertness. If he ever faced someone outside of his own court, his power would be weakened.

Cade walked a few feet behind Raith. The two had been close as children. Playing in the fields. Pranking the castle staff. Sneaking into the forest they were forbidden from entering. As the two grew older, the distance between them swelled. Cade knew Raith was jealous of him. His own mother had died, and Raith never accepted Cade's mother as his own.

Their father waited in the battle room in the training tower. His salt and pepper hair almost reached his shoulders now—a big change to the short hair he'd had when Cade was a child. He wore a gold crown atop his head.

Wrinkles had formed on his face. Such a rare occurrence for a high fae.

The walls of stone stood high in the large room. Swords, staffs, and other weapons hung on the far wall. The king stood in the middle of the room. His hands clung to his sides, and his eyes remained closed.

"My sons," he said, his voice weak. He turned to them and opened his eyes. The quick deterioration of the king was peculiar. Most high fae lived for centuries. A benefit of the magic that coursed through their veins was good health. Something had caused the king's health to dwindle, but no one had been able to determine what. Cade suspected it had something to with the Winter Court. Poison, perhaps. But it was nothing more than a guess.

Cade rarely saw his father lately. Spring was a quiet season for the Summer fae. The festivals and dances happened mostly in their respective season.

"Summer is here. Your battle will be the center of the Summer Festivities. Come closer." He motioned toward them.

Cade and Raith stepped closer. Both boys stood taller than their father, Cade the tallest of the three. Raith had steel blue eyes that matched their father's, while Cade had inherited his mother's. The King placed his hands on each boy's shoulder. "The Battle is inevitable, I know. As an only child, I was fortunate enough not to fight for the Right of Heir. But I never had the blessing of a sibling as you two do. I pray you remember that you will always be brothers."

The king had grown sentimental as his health decayed.

Hoping for a brotherly relationship between Cade and Raith was wishful thinking, but Cade wouldn't be the one to ruin a dying man's dream.

"Of course," Raith said as he mimicked his father's gesture. "The Right of Heir should go to the most capable. No hard feelings if my younger brother wins." Raith patted the king's shoulder. He grinned at Cade, and Cade knew that Raith had as little faith as he did that they would ever be as close as they once were.

The king took his hands back to his side. "The Festivities will start next week. You will both be obligated to attend each event. Each of you should spend most of your time training over the summer. You are each assigned a guide from my guard to help you prepare. Please restrain from any physical harm to one another, in the meantime." A twinkle flickered in his eye, reminding Cade of a younger version of his father. One he hadn't seen in a very long time.

"Certainly," Cade said.

A coughing spasm attacked the king, who excused himself to his bedroom to rest.

Cade saw Raith smirk as they left the battle room. "Laugh now, but I will defeat you."

Raith patted his brother on the back. "I expect you to try."

"My magic is stronger than ever," Cade said. Raith always underestimated him, patronizing Cade every chance he had. He would soon see that he'd been unwise to belittle his potential. "I have secrets that even you don't know."

After another chuckle, Raith replied. "So do I."

It had been a long time since they'd gotten along. So long, Cade had almost forgotten how it felt to have the brotherly love they once had. Or Cade had. He used to wonder if Raith ever loved him, but not anymore.

All that mattered now was preparing for the battle.

Cade's mother had spoken to him on his nineteenth birthday.

"You must challenge your brother. Your father is ill, and if something happens to him, I fear for our safety," she had said. "You are strong and far more of a leader than Raith." She spat out his name as if it were poison. His mother had little love for her stepson. As a child, Cade had tried to encourage the two to get along, but it hadn't worked. The more he tried, the more his mother disliked Raith. Eventually, he gave up.

Cade remembered the determination in her eyes when she told him he must challenge Raith. Even if he wasn't ready, he would do it. He couldn't disappoint her.

He must win.

Chapter Three

Raith watched his little brother hurry away, probably running to tell his mother about the meeting with the king. Cade was a momma's boy to the core.

Raith had no mother. Not anymore. She'd died long ago, and Raith had learned to take care of himself. His father had been seduced by Kassandra, the new queen. From the moment she had greeted the king at the Winter Ball, he was in trouble.

Kassandra was sweet to the eye, with long golden hair and icy blue-green eyes. But as Raith grew, he saw through her beauty. He sensed her greed. Her pride. Her jealousy. All the desires the king was blind to.

Within a month of their marriage, Kassandra held Cade in her womb. Raith was only five when Cade was born, and, for many years, he was the perfect big brother. When he was allowed to be around Cade, that was. Kassandra watched Raith closely. He felt her stare on him constantly. Even as a child, Raith was perceptive. He felt himself pushed out of the family as Kassandra tightened her grip on the king. But when Raith turned nineteen, his father had bestowed the Right of Heir to him. Even though it was custom to grant the oldest child the right, it angered Kassandra, which brought joy to Raith's heart.

Instead of going back to his room, Raith continued through the castle and out the back doors. The western sky faded from orange to purple to pink as the sun set behind the mountains in the distance. The back exit avoided the guards, who were nosy bastards that always wanted to know where he was going.

At least once a day, Raith made his way to the forest. Years ago, he'd placed a gate on the castle border wall so he could come in and out as often as he pleased. Kassandra complained it compromised security, but Raith had magicked the gate so only summer royalty could unlock it, so the king said it could stay.

Most fae from the castle feared the darkness within the woods. The forest had a mind of its own, stronger the deeper into the forest one would go. And magic. It could make people see things that weren't there. Feel things crawl on them. Hear snarls and howls. Of course, it could only do these things if you let it. Raith never did. The forest was full of trickery, but Raith's magic kept it from breaking into his mind.

As a Summer Court fae, Raith possessed mind powers. So did Cade, but they had different types of mind magic. Cade could enter dreams. He could use the emotion to refill his magic. Humans would wake up unaware that

Cade had been there. Raith's magic was different. He had access to memories—to see memories of others, to erase them, to share his own. The emotion in them fueled him as dreams did Cade. Raith could also use real life emotion like all high fae, the human-like fae who were the most powerful. The feeling of someone's emotion coursing through him was incredible, a high like no other. But he had other means to refresh his magic: nature.

His mother had taught him how to use nature to gain energy shortly before she died. She'd made him promise not to let anyone know what he could do—it was their secret. And an Autumn Court ability, as far as Raith knew. He wasn't sure how he could do it, but whatever the reason, he was glad. When he and Cade would sneak into the forest to play, he would use his magic in front of Cade, but he never shared its source. He kept his promise to his mother and never told another soul.

The castle courtyard was the only thing between the castle and the Summer Wood. Raith followed a stone path, passed a fountain, and then walked across grass until he reached a gate in the fence at edge of the forest. When his hand touched the gate's handle, it clicked open. As he stepped into the cover of the trees, his senses sharpened. His eyes adjusted to the darkness. He inhaled the crisp forest scent as he pressed further until he came to a tall tree that curved like a quarter moon. Its trunk was thick and rose high. At first glance, it looked like any of the other trees around. Bigger, perhaps, but just as tree-like. But a door was hidden in the moss-covered bark.

Raith swung the door open with his magic. Inside, a

ladder led down. He lit a candle at the top, shut the door, and climbed downward to a large room below the ground. More candles illuminated the room. On the far wall, a green blanket covered the bed. Close to the ladder, an oversized chair and ottoman sat, both charcoal in color. Raith walked across the wooden floor and over a braided rug. He closed his eyes and breathed deeply and a fire grew in the fireplace, sending warmth throughout the room.

This place was his and his alone. He'd never brought anyone here. Not Cade. Not any of the female fae he'd taken home to bed. On those nights, he went to his room in the castle, which was more impressive to them anyway. When Raith needed time alone, he came to this tree. Its coziness clothed him like a blanket. Here, he could think about anything without interruption. About his mother. About the upcoming battle.

He popped open a bottle of fae wine and poured a glass. As he sipped the berry-flavored beverage, a tingle ran through him. Raith sprawled out on the bed, leaning against the willow tree headboard.

Cade thought he would defeat Raith. He assumed that Raith didn't practice his magic enough. Maybe he thought Raith didn't *have* much magic. But Cade would soon learn just what Raith was capable of.

SCARLETT FOUND herself at the top of the hill again. Unlike yesterday, today the sun shined brightly. High in the sky, its rays heated Scarlett's skin. Today was the first day she made the trip alone. She hadn't spoken to Ashleigh since their fight. Ashleigh had locked herself in her room and had only come out to heat up a frozen dinner in the microwave. More than ever, Scarlett wanted to go to her mom's grave. Nope. As usual, her fear overpowered everything. What a lousy chicken. She hated it. It was weak, the complete opposite of what her mother—and life—had taught her to be.

As a child, she was brave.

She didn't know what she was anymore.

Pathetic. That was it. She was pathetic. It was a lousy thing to be, but she didn't know how *not* to be. The thought of facing her mother's grave made every ounce of logic inside her vanish. Her chest would tighten and a wave of nausea would wash over her. Every day, it was the same thing. Over and over. Maybe she should quit trying. Nothing had changed no matter how many times she'd gone to the edge of the hill. She always froze. But, despite her failures, she was stubborn. If she was too chicken to face her mother, she deserved to feel miserable until she could.

Since Ashleigh wasn't there, Scarlett didn't have to wait for anyone. She could just turn around and go back home. But nothing waited for her there, so she sat on the edge of the hill and viewed her mother's grave from afar. No one else was around. Birds chirped a melodious song —a private concert just for Scarlett. Her thoughts drifted to the dream she'd had. It had played over in her head all morning. She couldn't shake the feeling that it was something more than just a dream. She couldn't say why she felt this way, which was anything but reassuring. It made sense that her brain had played out a fantasy in her sleep. She hadn't even thought about guys since she found her mom. Soon after her mother's death, she quit dating and going to parties—even texting. The only person she talked to outside of school was her best friend, Natalie. Maybe her body was having guy withdrawals. But the dream felt too real to be some subconscious message.

Her mother had always sworn her hallucinations were real.

Scarlett shoved the thought away, shifting her musings back to the dream. Her body tingled when she thought of Cade's mouth on her neck. No matter what kind of boy mess she'd ever gotten herself into, she could always go to her mom for advice. How Scarlett missed her. There had never been anything they couldn't talk about. Even something as bizarre as Scarlett's dream. Her mom would tell her not to worry, dreams were just escapes from reality. She'd laugh and add that she'd had some crazy dreams herself, yet was completely convinced that the voices she heard were real. The ache crept back into Scarlett's heart.

The birds went silent. Something crunched behind her. She twisted her neck around. What she saw shocked her.

Cade.

The man who seduced her in the most peculiar dream of her life stood there, seemingly in the flesh, dressed in clothing from a different time period. Could she be dreaming again? She didn't think so.

Was she hallucinating?

"I feel your sadness," Cade said. "I know you don't know me, but I can help."

Scarlett thought about her dream. This was the same man, with the vivid eyes and compelling stature. Had her dream been a premonition? Was that better or worse than a hallucination?

Whatever it was, it was freaky. "Help me how?"

Her heart raced. She should get up and run away. Staying there alone was dangerous. No one could hear her if she screamed. But her body didn't move.

He closed the distance between them and reached for her hand. Something about him called to Scarlett, like a voice at the end of a long, dark tunnel guiding her where she needed to go. She didn't know Cade. If he was real, he could be a psychopath luring her away to murder her. Or a stalker. Her better sense told her to sprint home and lock the doors, but any sense she had stayed quiet as she her fingers took his.

His touch was warm, and, as his skin brushed hers, a wave of peace flowed through Scarlett. He smelled of lemon and pine. The pain she felt moments ago had vanished.

He pulled her to her feet.

"What are you?" she asked. Whatever it was, it couldn't be human. What else could he be? The thought alone was crazy.

"I'm someone who can keep your pain away." Not a real answer, but what did she expect? That he'd say he was an angel sent to save her? She didn't believe in such things.

But then, before today, she wouldn't have believed someone could make her feel as Cade did. Or make her not feel.

"What's your name?" Scarlett asked as Cade's fingers played with hers. Maybe her dream was wrong. How could she know the name of someone she'd never met?

"Cade."

The same name.

As crazy as the situation already seemed, she didn't want him to know she had dreamt about him.

Scarlett dropped his hand and stepped back. Her pain returned, like a punch to her gut. She breathed deeply. The way he controlled her feelings—like a drug—wasn't natural.

Her intuition had always been her strongest asset. The one time she'd ignored it, she was nearly taken advantage of in a car. Since then, she trusted her gut. Always. And her gut told her Cade wasn't just a vision, he was real, and she should be careful.

"Thank you, Cade, but I should go home," Scarlett said.

"Of course." He bowed. "My offer still stands if you change your mind, Scarlett." After her name left his mouth, he vanished.

She hadn't told him her name today.

What if she was wrong and he was nothing more than a hallucination—her grief driving her mad? It was far more likely than him not being human. He had just *vanished*. Was Scarlett going crazy like her mom?

AFTER HIS ENCOUNTER WITH SCARLETT, Cade's magic buzzed. Emotion was fuel to fae power. When he consumed it, the magic in him grew. Like food energized a body, emotion, among other things, invigorated fae magic. Cade had breathed in Scarlett's emotion like the scent of a candle; invisible but no less potent for its transparency.

He should feel sorry for the girl. So much pain couldn't be pleasant. But the more magic he had, the better he could prepare. Magic gave Cade strength. It helped him enter dreams. Helped him appear invisible and move things with his mind. With enough emotion, they could create energy into a weapon. Magic made the fae superhuman. Humans played their part. Their emotions refueled the fae. An angry man in a check-out aisle. A jealous girl at a high school dance. A grieving woman on the hillside of a cemetery. Each could feed Cade the sustenance his fae self needed. The stronger the emotion, the quicker he refueled and the more powerful his magic was.

Grief poured from Scarlett, a monsoon of pain. Gloom clouded around her as she fought the storm within. Cade couldn't vanquish her pain forever, but he could temporarily remove it from her mind as if it didn't exist. She'd have to deal with it again someday, but that would be her problem, not his.

Humans longed for a quick release from pain. It made them easy to lure into Faerie. *Never bring humans in against their will*—the rule of the Summer Court his father had put into place before Cade was born. Anyone found guilty of violating the rule would be killed. It was the highest law of the Summer Court.

There were six different fae courts, each with their own set of regulations. Four of them—one for each season—lived in Faerie. The other two wandered the mortal realm. Cade had learned about them all in his studies, but only bothered himself with Summer Court dealings. If he became king, that would have to change.

The fae weren't immortal, but many lived for centuries. Unlike humans, the fae had the blessing of good health. No colds, no measles, no cancer. Usually. Eventually, old age would catch a fae. Or a soldier might die in battle. But if careful, fae could live a long time.

The biggest risk of death for Cade was the upcoming battle.

To win, either he or Raith must defeat one another. By death or surrender, one of them would lose. To make the battle more intense, a surrender didn't have to be granted. It would be the champion's decision to spare the loser's life or to take it. With so much magic and emotion, many had killed their opponent without a second thought.

It was a danger Cade would face. What would the Summer Court become if Raith became king? The brother he knew as a child would have made a good ruler. He was protective and kind, not afraid to take the blame even if something wasn't his fault. But that Raith didn't exist anymore, and Cade worried what would happen to his mother if Raith got the Summer crown.

After Cade returned from his trip to the mortal realm, Kassandra was waiting for him outside of his bedroom.

"Mother," Cade greeted her.

Dressed in a long crimson gown, Kassandra curtsied. The gold crown covered in emeralds on her head didn't budge. Perfect posture, the sign of a true lady. Kassandra may have been raised outside of the castle, but her etiquette was very much that of a queen. Her days of working as a seamstress ended the moment the king took her hand to dance. She'd told Cade the story many times.

"It's time to step up your training. I've found a soldier from the army who is ready to leave as captain and return to the castle. An accomplished fighter that will serve as your trainer."

"Is a trainer necessary?" Cade asked. The magic inside him yearned for release. He'd never felt so full. Although he'd already practiced today, he was ready to go again.

Kassandra's eyes narrowed into a glare. The look of annoyance. Cade had seen it before, usually when he snuck around the castle as a boy, getting into things he shouldn't. "I would not have wasted my time finding this soldier if I didn't think it was necessary." She sighed and relaxed her forehead. "I know I ask a lot of you, my son. But I do not have royal blood, and if something happens to the king, the Heir will be given control of the realm. I fear what Raith might do if he were given this power. It's you who should be king."

Cade grabbed Kassandra's hand and squeezed it.

Once rough fingers were now as smooth as the satin of her dress. "I'll win."

"Don't be overconfident. No one expected Kaelem to become the Unseelie King, but it's he who now sits on the throne."

That cocky bastard didn't deserve to rule anyone. Then again, his brothers were arrogant jerks, too. But they were Unseelie fae, so what else would anyone expect?

"I've found a human who fills me with magic like I've never felt before," Cade said.

"Who is this human?"

"I don't know, but with her to feed off of, my magic will thrive." Cade cupped his hands together. A small orb of green light grew inside, blazing hot in his hands.

"Summer energy." Kassandra's eyes gleamed.

Cade nodded. It wasn't much—yet. But he was confident by the time the battle began, it would be a fierce weapon.

"Most don't gain that gift until years into adulthood." Kassandra's mouth shifted into a smirk. "Bring the girl here."

Chapter Four

S carlett wandered around town after Cade had scared her away from the hilltop. Zigzagging down blocks. Swinging in the park. Anything to pass time. She was in no hurry to get home. Would she and Ashleigh be okay? Would they just shake off their fight? Forget it happened? Or were they headed down a path that would tear them further apart than they already were?

She wanted to not care. It wasn't as if not speaking to her sister would kill her. But it hurt, and she felt more alone than ever. Perhaps that made her weak. But she didn't want to be alone. Was that so wrong?

She'd spent so much of her life with her mother, having time to herself felt foreign. Whenever she'd found time to get away, her mind still worried about her mom. Now, with Ashleigh not speaking to her, she had no one.

Growing up, sometimes she'd wished she had more time to herself. Being the younger sister quickly became bothersome. Teachers expected her to shine as brightly as Ashleigh had in their classes. They learned soon enough that she wasn't her sister. In fact, they were nearly opposite in so many ways. Ashleigh could sit at a desk for hours, attentively listening to every thing the teacher said as she took meticulous notes. Scarlett's mind wandered after the first five minutes.

She'd dream of far away lands where unicorns and princes existed. Places where the square root of a ten thousand didn't matter. It wasn't that she didn't want to be good like her sister, but it was so much harder for her. Even when she intended to go home and do her homework, life all too often got in the way. When her mother would be having a breakdown, chemistry seemed far less important.

She made the choices she thought were best, and now she'd been granted her wish; she was alone.

Sweat dribbled from Scarlett's forehead—the summer warmth in full effect, its thickness pressing into her. Her dry mouth begged for a drink of water, but she ignored it. She wasn't sure how long she'd been gone, but eventually her stomach grumbled and reminded Scarlett that she hadn't eaten since lunch the day before. Most of the time, she didn't even notice her hunger. Her thoughts were always elsewhere now. But the reality that she was human and needed food to survive caught up to her every so often. Scarlett checked her pocket for money, hoping to go to Paula's Cafe to get some chicken and fries. She didn't want to go back to her house and would avoid it as long as she could. But there was no money in her jeans, so home it was.

The sun dropped slowly in the eastern sky. Scarlett had been gone all day. It didn't feel like that long. Time had changed for Scarlett since her mom died. Some moments seemed to last forever, while others flew faster than a shooting star.

When she came through the front door, Ashleigh was curled on the couch watching TV.

"Hi," Scarlett said. She could be the bigger person.

"Hi." Ashleigh's gaze didn't budge.

"We okay?"

"Yep."

"Then why won't you look at me?"

Ashleigh's head snapped toward Scarlett. "Happy?"

"What can I do to make this better?" Scarlett and Ashleigh had never been close. But they were all the family each other had anymore. Scarlett didn't want to be alone.

"I'm going back to school tomorrow."

"You don't start for another month."

"Katie found an apartment for us but we have to start paying on it this month." Ashleigh shrugged. "So, I'm gonna head back and help her set it up."

"Fine." Scarlett couldn't believe Ashleigh would just leave. She'd already left Scarlett to handle everything the last two years while their mom was still alive. Why not just make Scarlett deal with everything else?

"You've always wanted your own space." Ashleigh

grabbed the remote and switched the channel to an America's Next Top Model rerun. "Now you'll have it."

"Awesome." Scarlett fought back the tears pooling behind her eyes. If Ashleigh didn't need her, she didn't need Ashleigh. Having a sister was overrated.

The piano in the corner of the room caught Scarlett's attention. A thick layer of dust covered it, dulling the brightness of the sage green paint underneath. She and her mom had painted it when Scarlett was in middle school. Its original wood had faded and wasn't worth saving and Scarlett wanted to make it her own, so she and her mom went to the store and bought a quart of paint—in whatever color Scarlett wanted—and borrowed a sander from the neighbor. Together, they gave the old piano a new life.

Scarlett hadn't touched it since she found her mom. She hadn't played it or even cleaned it. She'd dusted every other inch of the house, but she couldn't bring herself to do anything to the piano.

Staying home and sulking wouldn't make her feel any better. The walls around and empty feeling seemed claustrophobic. She needed to distract herself or she'd spend the entire night crying.

Scarlett would take her fate into her own hands.

She grabbed her purse and the keys to her mom's car and stormed back out the door.

She looked around the block. Had Cade followed her home? She didn't see him, thank god. The last thing she wanted to deal with was some supernatural freak of a creature. Or worse, a hallucination. Scarlett got in the car and drove to Natalie's. She blared the car radio to drown out the anger seething from her. Even though she didn't know the words, the thumping of the bass distracted her. At least she still had her best friend. Natalie lived across town. The benefit to living in a place so small was that you could get from one side to the other in a few minutes. Scarlett kept looking in her rearview mirror. Would Cade follow her? Did he drive? Scarlett doubted it, which made her even more nervous.

When she turned onto Natalie's block, she saw the group of cars parked in front. Scarlett recognized a few. Peter's Honda. Bailey's mom's van. Teddy's old Camaro. Teddy. He must be home from summer break. Scarlett's pulse jumped. She had barely talked to Teddy since Christmas time. The day she broke up with him. The shock in his eyes when she said it was over. He was the one good guy she dated and she blew it. No shock there.

Scarlett parked a few houses down. She used to just walk into Natalie's. They'd been friends since the first day of kindergarten. Practically sisters. Things got a bit awkward when Scarlett started seeing Teddy. He was Natalie's brother. Natalie wasn't happy when Scarlett suddenly ended it with no explanation, but a week later, when Scarlett found her mom's body, Natalie acted like nothing with Teddy had happened. Scarlett and Natalie, best friends again.

At first, when Natalie invited her to hang out, Scarlett did. They went to at least a party every weekend where Scarlett drank her pain away. A temporary fix, but a small respite was better than nothing. The last few months,

Scarlett kept to herself. During the week, she'd focused on school. On the weekends, she'd lost herself in a Netflix binge; any reality was better than hers.

It took Scarlett a minute to get the courage, but finally, she knocked on the door.

Natalie opened it with a beer bottle in her hand. "Oh my god, Scarlett. Are you okay?" She pulled Scarlett into a hug, seeming thinner than the last time Scarlett had hugged her. "Come in."

The front door opened into the living room. It was a small house, but the open floor plan made it seem bigger than it actually was. The room reeked of beer. A few people sat on the sectional. A few others, including Teddy, stood in the kitchen, his arm wrapped around a girl in a short, black skirt and heels. Her jet-black hair hit the middle of her back. Teddy laughed at something she whispered. His eyes crinkled like they always did when he smiled. He hadn't noticed Scarlett, yet.

"I'm okay," Scarlett said as she looked back to Natalie. "I can come back later. I don't want to interrupt."

"No, stay." Natalie grabbed Scarlett's hand and pulled her into the living room. "Look who came to join us." Natalie smiled. Still her outgoing self, though the bags under her eyes made her look tired. "I think this calls for a drinking game."

Teddy's grin disappeared when he saw Scarlett. She stared into his eyes. How could she say she was sorry with just a look? Natalie handed Scarlett a beer. It had been over three months since Scarlett had drunk—the last time she went to a party at Bailey's. Teddy was there with the school skank, who'd had her eyes on him since freshman year. Scarlett drank. A lot. So much, she spent all night in the bathroom, where Teddy found her and held her hair as she became one with the toilet. He didn't talk to Scarlett then, but he was there for her like he promised he always would be.

Breaking up with him was the right thing to do. He deserved better than Scarlett.

Scarlett gulped half the beer her first drink. It tasted as bad as it used to, but she knew too well how it felt after she drank enough.

Everyone gathered in the living room and played a game. Scarlett finished her first beer and started another, the buzz tingling her skin.

Ashleigh was right. Scarlett was a screw up. Why should she bother changing now? She was here with people who understood her. Might as well enjoy herself. Scarlett pressed the beer to her lips and chugged.

◈❦◈

WITH HIS FAE SENSES, Cade could find Scarlett as long as she didn't get too far away. If she stayed within a few miles, he could evanesce to her. When a fae fed on someone, a link was formed. Cade closed his eyes and reached for Scarlett's aura. Once he connected to it, his body became energy that moved through the air swiftly until it found its destination.

Cade had followed Scarlett to a small house at the edge of the human town. The house looked like every other house on the block. Single story. Tan in color. Worn out roofs. Nothing spectacular. But this house was fuller than the others. He could feel the alcohol buzzing inside.

Wearing an invisible glamour, Cade went around the house and through a gate. A German Shepherd growled at him from the back porch. Cade hissed and the dog whimpered. Humans bragged themselves the superior species, but they had the dullest senses. Cade opened the blinds of the sliding door with his magic and peeked inside. Past the empty kitchen, a group sat around a sectional with beers in their hands. Scarlett held a beer in one hand and with the other, tapped a finger on her thigh, her gaze pointed downward.

Cade inhaled her nervousness.

An idea came to him. Summer fae usually dressed more formal than the average human. Especially a prince like Cade. Normally he didn't use glamour for clothing. It was a hassle. Actually wearing clothes was easier and didn't require any magic. But showing up in the suit he was wearing would look too suspicious, so for tonight, glamour it was. He shifted his suit into jeans and a Pink Floyd t-shirt he'd seen before—a human enough outfit.

Cade knocked on the door.

"Guys, shhh," a voice said. "Hide the beer."

Cade chuckled. Humans and their laws. The Summer fae didn't drink beer, but they had their own kind of wine. All the fae enjoyed it, even the children. It fueled their powers. Made them happy. And it didn't have the bad habit of causing belligerent fighting like human alcohol.

All that human emotion fired up Cade's magic, so he wasn't complaining.

A short girl opened the door. "Can I help you?" Her blood shot eyes blinked at him. She kept her mouth shut, likely hiding the beer on her breath. If Cade were a cop, she had bigger problems to worry about. The whole house reeked.

"I'm Scarlett's friend." Cade smiled. He put his hands in his jean pockets. A nervous habit humans seemed to have. "Is she here?"

The girl eyed Cade from top to bottom and back to the top. His beauty always awed humans. Especially the girls. Insecurity radiated from her, which surprised Cade. She was pretty enough for a human. "Scarlett. Someone's here for you." The girl reached out her hand. "I'm Natalie."

Cade ignored her. He felt Scarlett as she approached. The pain in her chest mixed with the alcohol in her veins. Jealousy also coursed through her. An emotional mess. But a beautiful one. He'd been so consumed by her pain earlier, he didn't actually look at her. Her brunette waves hit the middle of her back. Freckles covered the top of her nose across her pale skin. When she saw Cade, her blue eyes doubled in size.

"Who's he?" Natalie asked.

"Cade." Scarlett replied. She kept looking at Cade and then back to Natalie. "What are you doing here?"

"I just wanted to check on you. See how you were feeling."

"I'm fine."

Natalie elbowed Scarlett in her side. "Invite him in." She winked.

Scarlett bit her lip. "Would you like to join us?"

"I thought you'd never ask."

When Cade walked in with Scarlett, envy boomed from a guy on the couch. Natalie introduced everyone. Jealous guy was named Teddy. He had his arm around a girl whose hand rode dangerously high up his leg. Cade placed his hand on Scarlett's lower back as he followed her through the living room. Anger radiated from Teddy. Cade winked at him and inhaled his fury. Humans were so easy.

Cade toyed with him even more by placing his own hand on Scarlett's lap after they sat down. Scarlett gazed at Teddy and then brushed her fingers with Cade's. She was drunk and flirty, and, even without his fae gifts, Cade knew she wanted to make Teddy jealous. He whispered into her ear. "You're beautiful."

Flattery worked wonders on humans, but it wasn't a lie. Scarlett was one of the prettiest humans he'd met. Her eyes held a fire, her face an innocence. An unusual combination and one that intrigued Cade. Her emotion tasted stronger than anything he'd had before.

Natalie brought Cade a beer. He thanked her and took a sip. Disgusting. Why would any creature willingly drink that awful beverage? Its fizziness burned his throat. Cade joined in on the drinking game they played, forcing him to sip his beer when the game dictated. Human alcohol was too weak to do much to Cade.

Scarlett's cheeks grew more flushed with every gulp of

beer she took. When Natalie got up to go to the kitchen and tripped over someone's legs, Scarlett burst into laughter. The alcohol had dulled her pain, but the jealousy radiating from her every time she looked at Teddy tasted delicious.

And the fury from Teddy whenever Cade touched Scarlett was savory, too. Cade ran a finger up Scarlett's leg. She giggled. Teddy fumed. Who knew spending time in the mortal realm could be so fun?

But Cade couldn't forget why he'd come here.

When he went home tonight, Scarlett would be by his side.

❧

MOST OF THE TIME, Raith ignored Cade's arrogance. But after speaking with the king, Raith wondered about the *secrets* Cade spoke of. When Raith woke Cade from his earlier dream, magic buzzed in the air. What had Cade found in the human world that brought him such power?

Raith followed Cade through a portal door and into the town of Silver Lake. The quaint town had a habit of luring the fae. When Raith was a teenager, he wandered around the town, watching the humans and their busy human lives. Doors in Faerie led to many different places around the human world. Japan, Sydney, New York. All had much more going on than Silver Lake. But there was something that hummed beneath its surface that drew the fae to come back time after time.

Once through the portal, Raith wandered around. He

passed the high school and its empty parking lot. A place he'd been before. A place where he did something he thought he'd never do: save a human.

But that was long ago. He hadn't visited the town in a couple of years.

After some time had passed, Raith closed his eyes and searched for his brother. Once the connection was made, Raith inhaled deeply. If his brother was nearby and his mental shields were down, Raith would be able to sense him.

There he was.

Eyes closed, Raith exhaled and felt for the location of Cade. His body fizzled into energy and transported itself to his brother. He'd evanesced himself outside a boring human house. His brother was inside. Why was Cade here? From the front yard, Raith explored inside the house with his magic. Alcohol, lust, jealousy. An explosion of emotion. Nothing more than the average rundown bar, though. Something else must have drawn Cade here.

Raith walked around to the back yard and peeked through the kitchen window. He saw the back of Cade, dressed in human clothing, with his arm wrapped around a human girl. What had gotten into his brother? Raith reached his magic to the girl. The rush he felt explained everything. She carried pain and turmoil so strong an electric pulse jolted through Raith. And something else Raith couldn't describe. This was the source of Cade's new confidence.

But Cade didn't know Raith had his own secret source of power.

Chapter Five

T he beer had soaked into Scarlett's stomach and taken control. The room spun around her slowly as she took another drink. She leaned into Cade and sank into his warmth. Even in her drunkenness, she realized that Cade was there and Natalie had acknowledged him. He wasn't just a hallucination. He was real.

She wasn't losing her mind. Well, she hoped not. At least Cade wasn't just a vision. Then again, he wasn't *human* either, and she wasn't sure if that was worse. What about her had piqued his interest?

Scarlett caught Teddy's gaze. Again. Ever since Cade showed up, he'd sent her dozens of glares. Scarlett giggled. She didn't even know what Cade was, but his body so close to hers felt right. It was much better than staring at Teddy and the bimbo with him.

Natalie knocked a lamp off an end table with her

elbow and burst into laughter. "I think," she hiccupped, "I have had enough." She propped herself up against the arm of the couch. "My dearest brother, help a sister out and take me to my room?" Natalie slurred.

Teddy sighed but left his date and held his sister upright as he helped her to her bedroom.

"Follow me," Cade whispered into Scarlett's ear. He lifted her with the arm that reached around her waist. Cade led Scarlett through the kitchen and to the back porch. The night wind sent a chill through Scarlett, but Cade pulled her closer. "Come with me, Scarlett."

She peered up into his aqua eyes. She wasn't sure if it was the beer or Cade's proximity that calmed her. The fight with Ashleigh, Teddy's new girl. Her mom's death. None of it seemed to matter anymore. It was unnatural how free she felt. It should scare her, but with her worries so far away, any uneasiness she should be feeling was miles away.

Scarlett closed her eyes and inhaled the freshness of the night. "Where will you take me?"

Cade tucked Scarlett's hair behind her ear and nibbled on her lobe. "To a castle, where you won't have to worry about all your *human* worries again."

A castle?

Scarlett placed her head on Cade's chest. Her pain had flown so far away, she barely remembered it anymore. What was the big deal, anyway? She was a screw up. No one was left to miss her anymore, and Cade brought her a peace she hadn't felt in such a long time.

Could she just leave her whole life?

"You'll be miserable without me." Cade pulled away from Scarlett. Emptiness stabbed her in the chest. The hole inside her returned and hurt more than ever.

Her chest tightened. An image of her mother, dead on the floor, flickered in her mind. She tried to think of her mother's smile, but she couldn't remember it. All she could see was the cuts up her mother's wrists and blankness in her eyes. Her mother's vacant expression fractured Scarlett's soul into a billion pieces.

Whatever it would take for it to disappear, she'd do.

"I'll go."

He wrapped his arms around her and she felt whole again, free from the painful memories.

A small part of Scarlett felt bad about leaving the party without saying goodbye. She could tell someone to let Ashleigh know she was leaving for good and was one less problem for her to worry about. Maybe even say goodbye to Teddy and wish him well. He deserved a goodbye. And Natalie, her best friend, would never know where Scarlett went. But as Scarlett walked, hand twined with Cade's, none of it seemed important enough to bother with. Together, they walked through town. Past the neighborhoods. Down main street. To the outskirts of town where trees towered, blocking the starlit night above.

In the woods, the crisp night air dropped even cooler. Something flowed through her veins. Something that was anything but worry.

"Are you ready?" Cade squeezed Scarlett's hand as

they approached an out of place wooden door. Floral iron accents surrounded its edges. The weathered wood felt old, like it was made a long time ago. Something else vibrated. It was as if whatever existed on the other side was a part of Scarlett. Like she belonged there.

The door stood alone in between two skinny trees. It didn't connect to anything and seemed rather pointless. "What's that?"

"An entrance to Faerie, the world of the fae." Cade put his hand on the doorknob. "Don't worry, you'll love it there."

A door that led to another *world*. Surely, this was a dream. If Natalie hadn't been able to see Cade, too, Scarlett would have sworn it was a hallucination. But somehow, it wasn't. She wasn't turning into her mom. Yet, at least.

The beer in her system caused Scarlett's head to spin again. Or maybe it was something else. She should think this through. Was running away really what she wanted? Cade placed his hands gently on the side of Scarlett's face and kissed her forehead and all her doubts vanished.

Cade opened the door. Behind it, Scarlett saw an empty room with stone walls. He held her hand and they walked through the door together.

There was no bang. No flash of bright light. No earthquake. Nothing out of the ordinary happened when Scarlett stepped through the door. And that was what made it creepy.

Yet, something changed *inside* her. Her skin tingled.

Iciness swam through her veins, then warmth. For a second, fire exploded inside her. She thought her heart might rupture. Then it cooled and she felt normal again. Normal-ish, at least. She couldn't place a finger on what had changed, but something had.

Once inside, Cade released Scarlett's hand. Worry crept back in.

She opened the door, only to find a wall of stone on the other side now, not the forest they had entered from. "Where'd Silver Lake go?"

"The door leads to many places and to nowhere at all." Cade grabbed Scarlett's hand again. "Don't worry, you're safe here."

A feeling of being trapped struck Scarlett, but, as if nothing more than a fleeting thought, the dread drifted elsewhere.

They left the empty room and entered a hallway. It was lit by white candles hung on the walls. Her feet clinked on the hard floor. The hallway seemed to go on forever, but before they reached the end, Cade stopped at a door. Inside was the most magnificent room Scarlett had ever seen. Crystal chandeliers lit by more candles hung from the ceiling. A canopy bed sat against the wall, with roses etched into its wooden columns and a sheet of velvet draped above. A large fireplace across from the bed lit magically.

"Did you do that?" Scarlett asked Cade.

"Yes." Cade wrapped his arms around Scarlett. "There's a lot I can do."

Scarlett leaned into Cade. She wanted to know the things Cade could do.

As her nerves settled, curiosity took hold. Scarlett had always wished for her life to be different. She'd felt in her soul that there was more out there somewhere.

This place was just that.

Chapter Six

So, his baby brother had found a human magic fountain. No big deal. Raith didn't need humans for power. Still, he couldn't deny he was curious about this girl. Why was her emotion so potent? Raith didn't have time to dwell on it, though. He was late for his first battle practice.

Raith had spent the night in the castle. He preferred the solitude of his tree, but since the battle was nearing, he worried someone would discover his spot. It wouldn't surprise him if Kassandra sent one of her minions to spy on him. To protect her *baby*, Cade. Raith rolled his eyes at the thought. For as worthless as Kassandra made Raith think he was, he knew she was worried. In her mind, the Summer Court would simply fall apart if Raith were king. Or maybe that wasn't her worry. Maybe she worried he would make a great king, but she knew he'd make her pay for the way she'd treated him growing up, excluding him from the family every chance she got.

49

At first, he thought he'd just train on his own. He didn't need some soldier from the royal guard to teach him. If the soldier were so powerful, he wouldn't be spared from his guard duties. Not that there any much threat to the Summer Court. It hadn't been attacked by anyone since long before Raith was born. But you can never be too prepared, or so Kassandra always told the king. She made more of the royal decisions than he did.

After climbing three flights of stairs, Raith arrived at the training tower and entered one of the smaller training rooms. Weapons covered the circular stone walls of the room. Swords, staffs, bows and arrows. Any weapon the summer fae had ever known was in this room. There were no guns. Shooting something so fast and powerful from far away was for cowards, or so the War Council had decided when humans invented them. Guns, cannons, and bombs were banned. If any fae tried to sneak them into the realm, they would vanish. The realm had powers of its own. Sometimes a mind of its own, too.

As a child, Raith and Cade had fighting lessons. Cade always chose a sword, the typical choice. Their father's preferred weapon. Raith favored daggers. Their versatility. Their stealth. The feeling of their slash through the air, sharp and quick. They'd be allowed one weapon for the final battle. Daggers would be Raith's choice. He didn't want Cade to know, though. So he would practice with all the weapons. One thing Raith learned long ago was never trust anyone. His trainer could be under the grasp of the queen—feeding her information about Raith's strengths and weaknesses. Or maybe he would be on Raith's side. It would be a first, though, so Raith would be careful.

He grabbed a sword from the wall, its shiny metal glistening in the sunlight sneaking through a window. It felt clunky in his hands as he waved it through the air. He twirled it behind him and it grazed his side.

"Watch where you're swinging that thing," a deep voice said behind him. "I'm Jaser, your trainer."

This guy couldn't be more than a few years older than Raith. He had dark brown hair, with chocolate eyes and caramel skin. Apparently, someone experienced was too much for Raith. Figured. At least he gave the whole trainer thing a chance. Raith hung the sword back up and made for the exit.

"Leaving so soon?" Jaser asked.

"I don't need a trainer," Raith said as he walked through the door. A whizzing sound passed his ear as a dagger flew into the wall in front of him and clinked on the ground.

"Your brother wouldn't have missed on purpose."

Raith snatched the dagger. "I wouldn't have turned my back on him." He tossed it to Jaser, who caught it in the holster attached to his pants.

"You should be as prepared as possible before the battle."

Even though he was younger than Raith expected, Jaser might be worth more as a teacher than he'd thought at first glance. Still, he wasn't in the mood to train today.

"Maybe next time you can enlighten me with your wisdom." Raith turned away, heading straight for his tree.

Chapter Seven

A bright light shone through the window and into Scarlett's eyes, stirring her awake. Her body sank into the mattress as she hugged the warm blankets covering her. She couldn't remember the last time she had slept so well. Lately, she'd barely even slept. Last night was a dreamless night. For the first time in a long time, Scarlett woke rested.

Her eyes blinked as they adjusted to the brightness. The first thing she noticed was the velvet, turquoise canopy above her head, accented with silver swirls, hung from a large, four-poster bed.

It wasn't in her bed and she wasn't in her own clothes. She wore a long, pale pink nighty.

Scarlett thought back to the night before. Her fight with Ashleigh, the party, and Cade. She remembered the lightness she felt when she was with him. She also remembered leaving her realm and entering his.

She was in a different *realm*. What had she done?

Alone, her brain felt clearer. The emptiness inside her thrummed. Not only had she lost her mom, but now her sister didn't even want to speak to her. She was probably better off in a different realm. Maybe her sister would regret blaming Scarlett for everything. Or maybe she'd be glad Scarlett was gone. Either way, Scarlett was somewhere else now. She may never see her sister again.

The idea should freak her out. Maybe she'd read too many vampire stories, but she wasn't surprised that a whole other world existed. There had been times she'd see someone lurking that others paid little attention to. Scarlett could feel something different about them, but she couldn't say what exactly. She didn't want people to think she was a freak. *Like her mom.* The thought punched Scarlett, but it was true. To most of the world, her mom's visions of people who weren't there and erratic behavior made her crazy. What made Scarlett think her sense about people was any different? Now she wondered if she'd been right all along.

This world was far more luxurious than the one Scarlett was from. The room she was in came straight out of the fairytale book Scarlett's mother read to her as a child —when she was on her medication, that was. Scarlett had always loved fairytales. The gold walls had dark wainscoting, and candles littered the room, though none were burning.

As a child, Scarlett wanted to be a princess swept off her feet by Prince Charming. When she got older, she quit reading the tamed versions and moved to the darker ones. Where Sleeping Beauty was raped by a king. Cinderella's sister cut off her toe to fit into the slippers. And the evil queen in *Snow White* was forced to dance in burning hot shoes until she dropped dead. Actual life was messy. Fairytales should be, too. Prince Charming didn't come to the rescue. Throwing a penny in a wishing well didn't make your dreams come true. She would know.

Scarlett pulled the silk sheet up to her shoulders. The soft material slid against her skin. She closed her eyes and sank her head into the feather pillow. It smelled like lavender. She wasn't a princess, but she would enjoy this moment as if she were.

"Morning." Cade entered the room. Today's outfit was very different than yesterday's. At the party, he looked like any other of the guys there. Today, he looked like a sixteenth century prince, in black boots and pants and a long, black leather coat with gold accents. "Peony will be in to help you get ready."

"Ready?" Scarlett sat up in the bed. "For what?"

"To meet my mother."

Meet his mother? That seemed quite a big step after one night. They didn't even do anything but sleep. Cade put his hand on her shoulder. Scarlett's nerves faded.

"Don't worry. My mother just likes to meet any humans I bring into Faerie."

A woman, dressed in a modest gray dress, entered the room. Unlike Cade, her ears were round like Scarlett's. She must have been human.

"This is Peony. She will find you a dress and help you bathe."

Peony curtsied to Cade as he left. Her long silver hair was pulled into a bun. "Come," she said and then went through a door in the corner of the room.

Scarlett shivered when she got out of the bed. She rubbed her arms as she followed Peony into the largest bathroom she'd ever seen. Marble covered the floors. The claw foot tub underneath the stained-glass window could fit three of Scarlett into it. Peony turned on the bath water. She left the water running and stood next to Scarlett. She held out her hand. "Your nightgown, Miss."

Now Scarlett really felt like a princess. Someone to run her bath water and take her clothing from her. Scarlett pulled the nighty over her head and handed it to Peony. Her nakedness made her modest, but Peony didn't pay any attention. Scarlett waited until the bathtub was half full and then stepped inside. The hot water warmed her as she sank into it. She relaxed as the tub filled, then Peony helped her wash her hair and back. It was a strange combination of awkward and wondrous. As Peony rinsed the soap off of Scarlett's shoulders, Scarlett asked, "You're a human, right?"

"Yes, Miss." Peony poured water on Scarlett's neck.

"And you help Cade?"

"I belong to Miss Kassandra."

"Cade's mom?"

"Yes."

Belong. A strange word to use. Peony didn't work for her. She belonged to her. Like a slave? Scarlett wanted to ask more, but she didn't want to offend Peony. What did Cade want from Scarlett?

After she finished the bath, Peony wrapped Scarlett in a plush towel. "I'll be right back, Miss."

While Scarlett waited, she looked at her reflection in a mirror on the wall. Her long hair waved from its wetness. The water had washed away her makeup. The bags that had been under her eyes had halved in size since yesterday thanks to the full night of sleep. Her skin appeared brighter than normal, and, her irises seemed to have the slightest purple tone. Peony returned and helped Scarlett into a floor length mauve dress. Sparkles covered the bust. Scarlett sucked in as Peony tightened the corset.

The bottom of the dress brushed the floor as Scarlett walked back to the bedroom. Peony gestured for Scarlett to sit on the bed, and then she put a pair of gray heels on Scarlett's feet.

"How long have you been here?" Scarlett asked.

"With Miss Kassandra?"

"Here in this realm."

"For three years."

Peony moved on to Scarlett's hair. She brushed out all the tangles. "I'm not crazy, like I'm sure you're thinking," Peony said. "My old life wasn't worth living. Miss Kassandra takes my pain from me, and I serve her in return."

What could be so bad that being a servant was the better option? If Cade would take away all Scarlett's pain, would she do whatever he asked? She hoped not.

And what exactly did he expect of her?

Scarlett thought of her mother. She wished more than anything to have her mother back again. That wasn't possible, though, and she couldn't even think of her mom without a tightening in her chest. If Cade could take that away, Scarlett wasn't sure she could say no.

Great, the stab in her chest was back.

Once Scarlett's hair was twisted into a bun, Peony dabbed some makeup on her face. Soon after, Cade was back to escort Scarlett to meet Kassandra. As soon as he stepped in the room, her pain dulled.

"You look lovely," Cade said as he locked his elbow with Scarlett's.

They walked arm in arm down the hall. Scarlett admired the pictures that hung on the wall. Most were portraits of beautiful beings, but some were of trees and rivers and other landscapes. After climbing a staircase, they went down another hallway and arrived at Kassandra's room.

A man with a sword at his belt stood outside the door.

"We're here to see my mother," Cade said.

The man stepped aside and let them enter. This room was even larger than the room Scarlett had been in. On the far side, a large window covered over half the wall, from the floor to the tall ceiling. A woman, who Scarlett guessed must be Kassandra, lounged on a chaise in front of it.

"Dearest son," she said in a smooth voice as she stood. "Who have you here?" Kassandra wore a metallic dress that was neither gold nor silver, but a shade in between. The bust pushed up her breasts, which were framed in a square neckline and puff sleeves. A gold crown sat atop her head.

Scarlett curtsied. Or tried to curtsy, at least. She'd never had to be so proper before. Hopefully curtsying was normal here. Kassandra returned the curtsy with one herself. Scarlett relaxed.

Cade released his arm from hers and stepped away. "Scarlett, meet my mother, the Summer Queen."

The Summer Queen? It made sense—Scarlett was in a castle after all. But to meet some inhuman queen took Scarlett's breath.

Kassandra was lovely, with flawless peach skin. Her sea-green eyes were stunning, but cold. A shudder tingled Scarlett's spine. As beautiful as the queen was, she looked dangerous.

Kassandra approached. She closed her eyes and breathed deeply. "Why yes, she is potent."

Potent? What did that mean? Kassandra ran the back of her fingers across Scarlett's cheeks, sending a shiver down her arms. Normal people didn't touch other people like they were pets, and right now Scarlett felt more like a dog than a person. Peony was a human and she was a servant. Something told Scarlett that humans weren't on the top of the food chain in Faerie.

"Such lovely skin." Kassandra twined her fingers through a strand of Scarlett's hair that had escaped from the bun. "And what dark hair."

Scarlett clenched her jaw, her teeth grazing the tip of her tongue. The tang of iron grazed her taste buds.

When Kassandra moved back to the chaise, Cade returned to Scarlett's side.

"She will be quite well for you, son."

Cade nodded and guided Scarlett back out of the room.

Whatever just happened, she needed to be careful.

Chapter Eight

Scarlett had met a fae queen and she wasn't sure if she should be flattered or petrified. The way Kassandra had spoken of Scarlett like she wasn't even there sent a queasiness to Scarlett's stomach. And she'd *pet* her.

Anytime fear or dread surfaced in Scarlett's mind, it slipped away before she could think too much into it.

"I told you my mother would approve," Cade said as he sat on the bed that would now be Scarlett's.

"What did she have to approve of?" Scarlett asked.

Cade gestured for her to sit next to him, and so she did. He rested his hand on her knee. He flicked his other hand and the door swung shut. "My mother is protective of me. You don't need to worry."

Before Scarlett could reply, Cade's hands moved to her face. He gripped her cheeks gently and pulled her mouth to his.

Scarlett pulled away. "This place seems…" She wasn't sure what to say without making things worse. "Different. Maybe you should take me home."

Cade sighed. "I didn't want to do this, but…"

The pain in Scarlett's chest hit her like a horse's hoof to her heart. Visions of her mother lying on the ground, the color drained from her face played through Scarlett's mind. The metallic smell of blood filling the room. The fight they had when Scarlett snuck into the house past curfew the weekend before her mom died. The disappointment in her mom's eyes.

It was too much. She needed it to stop. Scarlett grasped her stomach as she tried not to puke. She thought it hurt before, but that was nothing. These memories were a poison to her blood, spreading through her veins and making her sicker than she'd ever felt before. Her head spun. Her heart pulsed. Every muscle in her body ached. She couldn't live like this.

"Make it stop," Scarlett screamed. The memories loosened their grip. She looked into Cade's eyes and saw no remorse. She sensed the danger she'd put herself in by coming to this place with him, but it was a mistake she couldn't undo. He touched her lips with his finger. Her brain grew numb.

"You'll like it here. Promise. Just give it time." Cade's hand grazed Scarlett's thigh.

His lips met hers. A tingle spread through her face. Whatever had just upset her seemed light years away. Scarlett reached around Cade's back and pulled herself closer to him. The desire to be close to him overwhelmed her. She'd craved the touch of someone before, but never like this. This wasn't normal. Or human. It was something else. Something dangerous.

Scarlett was Cade's for the taking.

⚜

WHEN YOUR MOM HEARS VOICES, you grow up fast, or that was the case for Scarlett. Maybe if she'd had a dad there to help it would have been different. But it was just Scarlett, Ashleigh, and their mom.

Scarlett learned to pack her own lunches for school at six years old, asked her friends' moms for rides to and from softball practice after school, and even taught herself to drive.

And, maybe because she took care of herself all too often, she craved attention from guys. Or maybe she just liked how they seemed drawn to her—her bright eyes and flirty grin.

She'd tease them as they ogled her. For once in her life, she was in control of something. They would go only as far as she felt comfortable—never all the way. She wasn't a prude, her virginity not on some pedestal, but whenever she got close to crossing the line, she pulled back. None of the guys actually *knew* her. They thought she was pretty, sure, but until she dated Teddy, none of her boyfriends actually cared much about her.

She always had the control, until one night when a guy decided her consent wasn't important. She was trapped underneath him in his beat-up Chevy truck when someone pulled him off her and told her to leave.

She listened, running four blocks back to Natalie's, indebted to a stranger.

But now, under Cade's influence, her virtue was the last thing on her mind.

Chapter Nine

C ade left Scarlett's room with a smirk on his face. Magic buzzed though him. Scarlett's pain was feast enough, but the lust she radiated filled him even more. He had to use it wisely, though. For his own desires, he wanted to devour her fully, but her hunger for him would last longer if they took things slowly. Kisses would have to do for now.

She was his to command. Mortals—so driven by emotion—were easy prey. With the right technique, he could control her. Her will would bend to him and she wouldn't even know it. With the Summer Court law, humans had to enter Faerie willingly, but once they were there, there was no regulation from using his fae gifts to keep them.

Scarlett would do as he wished for as long as Cade needed her. Once he won the battle, he could be kinder. Until then, he would do what he must.

It was time for Cade's first official training session. He'd been preparing over the last couple of months by himself, but once the battle was declared, each competitor was assigned a mentor to train him.

Cade entered the training tower and went into the battle room where his father had met him and Raith. A girl dressed in a brown fighting suit, with a long blonde ponytail that fell to the middle of her back, looked out the window and onto the courtyard. The open window allowed a breeze to sweep through the room.

"You're late," she said as she turned to him. Her silver eyes glared at him.

"You're a girl," Cade said. He was expecting some burly, fae warrior to be waiting for him, not some scrawny blonde girl.

"A *woman*, to be correct." She approached him. "Got a problem with it?"

She was a pretty girl, at least. She might not be so bad, he thought, until she slugged him in the stomach.

Cade bucked over as he held his gut, his breath stolen.

Her eyes narrowed. "I am the top graduate from last year's battle class, and I don't appreciate you ogling me."

Cade straightened up. "Fine."

"I'm Poppy," she said. "And I know you're Cade. Nice to meet you. Blah, blah."

No one had ever been so direct toward him. He wasn't sure if he was offended or impressed.

"Pick a weapon," Poppy said.

He wanted to storm out of the room to prove no one

told him what to do, but he swallowed his annoyance. *After* he became king, he wouldn't listen to anyone he didn't want to listen to. Until then, he'd begrudgingly follow the girl's orders.

Cade browsed the weapon wall. He grabbed a sword. He loved the feeling of the weight in his hands.

"Typical." Poppy grabbed an iron staff. "The sword is a classic, and, when used right, powerful. Now, let's face each other and practice."

At least she didn't waste any time.

Cade swung the sword at her throat. Maybe that would shut her up. Her staff met the sword and pushed it back toward Cade. As he veered it back at Poppy, she twirled her staff above her head and around Cade's body, and then hit the back of his knees, knocking him to the ground.

"It's also heavy and clunky, and, if you don't control it properly, a liability."

This Poppy was going to drive him crazy before he even made it to the battle. She reached her hand out to help him up, but he ignored it and pushed himself from the ground.

"You can be as mad as you want, but don't think your brother's trainer isn't teaching him all of this, too."

"Since when do they allow girls into Battle School?"

"Since the General had a daughter."

The General's daughter? Cade's father had made his best friend the general when he became king. He was infamous for killing the Winter King and earning the Summer

Court victory in the recent war. Cade didn't know he'd had any children.

"Let's try again," Cade said. He didn't like losing. Surely, she'd just been lucky. He was ready for her now.

The second time, he lasted on his feet for a few minutes before Poppy knocked him down. She was too damn quick. How did someone so small have so much strength?

"Better already," she said.

Cade bit his tongue.

The longer they practiced, the dryer Cade's mouth became.

Poppy had barely worked up a sweat.

"You have to push past the fatigue." Poppy swung the staff into Cade's stomach.

"I'm *trying.*" He lunged at her, slicing his sword at her throat.

She hopped out of the way and brought her staff into his back.

After an hour of Cade getting knocked down over and over, she declared practice over.

"Hang in there, prince. You'll get it."

Losing was bad enough, but getting his ass kicked by a girl made it worse. What if the kingdom found out he couldn't even overpower a puny blonde? How would they trust him to rule the kingdom?

If he didn't beat Raith, he wouldn't have to worry about it. But this had been combat practice. He hadn't used any of his Summer energy. He'd like to see Poppy have beaten him if he had.

As Cade left training, a scroll tied with red ribbon appeared in front of him. He opened the note. *Come see me* was scribbled in cursive, signed by the queen. He groaned. He was tired and sweaty and needed to rinse off. He was a prince, not a servant to be summoned whenever his mother wished.

Despite his annoyance, he went to find her.

He wasn't sure where she'd be at this time of day, but he headed to the parlor. Sure enough, Kassandra sat at the pearl colored, grand piano.

"Music has never been my calling," she said as she twisted around on the bench. "My sister stole all that talent in the family."

"My trainer is a girl," Cade said. Surely, his mother would be able to fix it.

Kassandra laughed. "Of course, Cade. I am the one who assigned her."

"You assigned a girl to prepare me for the battle?"

Kassandra rose from the bench and waltzed to the couch placed underneath the room's large window. "I'll pretend to ignore the disgust in your voice. Don't forget your mother is also a *girl*."

"You're a wonderful woman, mother." Cade bowed to her. "I just assumed that someone with more experience would be better suited to train me."

"Poppy was in the top of her graduating class. She isn't as big as the other warriors, but she's smart. How else could she take down men twice her size?" Kassandra crossed her legs and placed her hands on her knee. "Your father is ill. He's hung on such a very long time, but I don't know that he will last much past the battle. I believe he wants you to be his successor, so he's holding on until you can win."

Cade doubted it. Father had always had a soft spot for Raith. As a child, Cade was sure that his father favored Raith over himself. It wouldn't surprise Cade if his father died the day before the battle blessing, the official commencement of the Right of Heir, so Raith would be king forever and Cade would have no chance to challenge him for the crown. Unless Raith was killed, in which case, the crown would pass to Cade, with or without their father's blessing.

Kassandra continued. "Things will be changing soon, my son. And Poppy will be a huge ally to our cause, so play nice."

Cade didn't know they had a *cause*. And what type of change was she talking about? "Change?"

"Don't worry about that, yet. You just focus on winning the battle." Kassandra patted the empty spot next to her. "Come sit."

It was unusual for his mother to be talkative. Cade joined her on the couch. His legs had already begun to ache from the training session.

Kassandra dismissed the guards and asked them to shut the door.

"How is Scarlett doing here?" Kassandra spoke quietly.

"Fine." Why all the secrecy? Scarlett was just a

human. Her emotion was delicious—sure—but she was nothing that out of the ordinary.

"And you're still gaining your fae energy?"

Cade hadn't tried to produce it lately, but when he focused, a teal orb grew in his hands, filling his palms. It was twice the size as the last time he'd generated it.

Kassandra grinned. "Wonderful. The more power you bring to the battle, the better. We have waited a long time for this. Keep focused, and don't let the girl go home."

Cade didn't plan on it, but he wasn't sure why his mother cared so much. "I can always find a human to bring here. There are plenty who want to escape their world."

"There's something different about Scarlett. I don't know what it is, yet, but if she fills your magic supply like you say she does, then she's to stay."

"Yes, mother." Cade said.

Kassandra cradled Cade's face in between her soft hands. "You must win this battle Cade. No matter what it takes. The Summer Court cannot go to your brother."

Cade nodded. He would out train Raith and use Scarlett to replenish his magic until he became king. After that, he would make the rules.

"You can go." Kassandra shooed him with her hand.

He stood and, with exhausted legs, walked back to his room to see Scarlett.

But she wasn't there.

RAITH HAD SPENT the day in his room in the castle. He folded the note in his hands as small it would go. It was a reminder of his scheduled battle practice. The soldier just couldn't take a hint. What about Raith leaving last time did he not understand?

As much as Raith didn't like the idea of someone else telling him what to do, he hated the idea of his little brother beating him in battle even more. While Raith *might* be able to waltz into the battle untrained and humiliate Cade, he also might show up unprepared and get his ass handed to him. He knew Cade well enough to know that Cade would attend all of his training sessions, extra even. His little brother was anything but unpredictable, a golden boy to his core.

With a groan, Raith headed to his training session. In the tower, Jaser swung a staff around the training room.

"Look who decided to bless me with his presence," Jaser said as he hung the staff on the wall. He approached Raith, who lingered in the doorway.

Jaser towered over Raith a few inches and had a sturdy build. He looked young, but Raith couldn't deny the fierceness he carried.

Well, he was already there. Might as well give Jaser a chance.

"What amazing things can you teach me?" Raith stared at Jaser, noticing a scar sliced across his right hand.

Jaser pulled his sleeve down to hide it.

Raith thought of his own scar, just above his left eyebrow—not as easy to conceal.

"Lesson one: never underestimate. Anyone. Ever." Jaser searched the weapon wall until he found a small dagger in between a bow and staff. "Or any weapon." He flung the dagger into a chest on the other side of the room, its tip piercing the wood. "Death comes from precision, not size."

Jaser explained all the weapons to Raith, their uses and downfalls, the best time to use each. At first, Raith pretended to listen. Then he found himself enthralled by Jaser's words. Raith hadn't expected to care about the history of each weapon, but he was fascinated. He'd learned about Summer Court history as a child, but his teacher's lessons were dry and boring. Passion radiated from Jaser as he spoke. Raith tried to act nonchalant, but Jaser smirked.

"Summer defeated Winter with this blade here." Jaser grabbed a bronze-headed spear from the wall.

"It's not even made with summer magic," Raith said.

Jaser twirled the spear through the air. "Nope. The General got mad and chucked it over the Winter front line and it shot right through the Winter King. He didn't even see it coming."

"Ouch."

No wonder the Winter Court wasn't too fond of the Summer.

"That'll teach a king to be in the middle of the battle. I don't know what he was thinking."

"So, they just surrendered?"

"His daughter was only fourteen. She wasn't ready to

be a Queen," Jaser said. "Summer would have won anyway. It was only a matter of time."

"Moral of the story: always watch for spears," Raith said. "Got it."

"That'll do for today," Jaser said as he hung the spear up. "Tomorrow we'll start to practice."

"How'd you get stuck as my trainer?" Raith asked. Jaser was far too knowledgeable and talented to be behind the scenes as a teacher. Usually retired soldiers taught, not young, healthy ones.

Jaser shrugged. "Captains don't like to lose." He smirked. "Plus, the way I see it, training you is more important than standing guard at a post that never gets attacked."

Raith wondered what the story behind Jaser and the captain was. Sometime he'd have to ask about it. Jaser seemed likable, and Raith didn't like a lot of people. He wasn't ready to let his guard down yet, but he was surprised to admit he may have been wrong. Jaser didn't seem like someone to get latched under Kassandra's fingers. Maybe Raith *could* trust him—only time would tell. If he wanted to win the battle, he might have to.

For now, Raith wanted to go back to his tree to relax.

"See you tomorrow then."

Maybe training wouldn't be so bad after all.

After the history lesson, Raith headed through the castle entryway to his tree.

"I just need to go outside," he heard a female voice say. A young woman pleaded with one of the guards at the front entrance. "It isn't a big deal."

A guard stood on each side of the tall iron doors of the castle. One guard kept his position, the other turned to speak with the girl.

Raith admired her from the back. She was tall for a girl, with curves in all the right places. With her hair pulled up, her long neck was exposed.

"No human is to leave without a fae. Queen's orders," the guard replied.

The girl sighed and turned her head. Raith recognized her immediately—the human Cade had found. He must have convinced her to come to Faerie somehow. Not surprising—Raith had felt her pain when he spied on them through the window. If Cade offered to take it from her, it was no wonder she came with him.

"There you are. I've been looking all over for you," Raith said. She would have no idea who Raith was, but he hoped she'd catch on and play along.

Her sky blue eyes widened when she saw Raith, but she was smart enough to act like she knew him. "I was *trying* to tell these guards that it's okay for me to go outside. You don't mind, do you, dear?" She grinned and hurried to Raith.

He locked his arm with hers. When their skin touched, a flicker of a memory flashed in Raith's mind. She stood atop a hill, staring down onto a graveyard. Fear filled the memory, and guilt.

It had been a long time since a memory had attacked him like that. Since he'd learned to control his gift, he only looked into minds when he wanted to. Why was this girl different?

"We'd like to take a stroll through the courtyard," Raith said to the guard, who stepped aside.

Cade must not have told the guards about the girl, yet. Otherwise they'd have known she was here with him, not Raith.

Raith led her outside. After the doors shut behind them, the girl pulled away.

"Thanks for your help," she said as she hurried down a path enclosed by rose bushes on each side.

"Where do you plan to go?" Raith asked. The front gate to the castle grounds was locked. And if she somehow made it past, humans couldn't make it far from the castle without being stopped. If they did, they'd be in even bigger trouble. The forest was no place for mortals.

"Home."

"I'm not sure how much you know about the Summer Court, but you're not going to make it home by walking."

The girl sighed and turned back to Raith.

"*You* could take me home." She smiled. A smart girl, using flirtation to wield Raith. Well, trying to.

"I don't even know your name."

"Scarlett."

"And how does a love like yourself end up here?"

Scarlett hesitated. Raith wondered if she'd mention Cade, if she even knew who he was here or why she agreed to come with him.

"I was tricked. Sort of. Mostly drunk."

At least she was honest. Some humans claimed they were forced, but the realm wouldn't let him in unless they agreed willingly. It didn't matter if they were intoxicated or coerced, though. Any verbal agreement counted.

Raith tasted her emotions. They had been bursting from her when he saw her in the human realm. Today, they had dulled, but pain still lingered on her skin. Cade had already fed from her, Raith could tell. If he guessed right, Cade had drained her completely not long ago. A void would linger after a human's emotions had been drained. It would fill back up eventually, but it would take time. Raith was surprised this girl had the determination to leave. Most humans took days to replenish themselves.

"Who brought you here?" He knew the answer, but he wanted her to answer him.

"Okay, look, I made a mistake. I was weak, and I agreed to come here because I thought it was a good idea. It doesn't matter who brought me, I just need to leave."

"Why don't you ask whoever brought you to take you back?"

Scarlett's forehead creased. "I don't think he'll take me."

This girl was worried, and she should be. Cade had found a brimming source of power. A jackpot for the upcoming battle. Raith could ruin it. He could take her back, help her hide, and Cade would have to find someone else.

"Scarlett." Cade yelled from the doorway, a scowl on his face.

Raith had taken too long. Shit. Cade had found her and would take her back to his room.

Scarlett pleaded with Raith one last time with her big

eyes. When he didn't respond, she groaned and stomped to Cade.

Another opportunity was sure to present itself. Raith would just have to wait.

He had to admit, this girl intrigued him, too.

Chapter Ten

❧

Cade rushed through the front door. Scarlett and Raith stood together, too close for his liking. A trickle of fury set his brows. He exhaled, releasing the tension.

How did Raith find Scarlett? If there was anyone he wanted to keep Scarlett from, it was him. His brother would steal her for nothing more than a laugh.

When Cade called her name, she walked to him. Raith followed her.

"I've been worried," Cade said as he kept his anger down. Letting his irritation show would only fuel his brother.

"You caught me," Raith said. "I stumbled upon Scarlett here and thought she deserved to see more of the castle than your bedroom."

"A great idea, but I can take it from here."

Scarlett looked back and forth between the brothers. Raith stared at Scarlett. Cade could sense curiosity from

Raith. A fae could read another fae if his mind shields weren't in place, and right now, Raith's were slightly lowered.

"Very well, brother." Raith bowed to Scarlett. "It was nice to meet you, love. I'm sure I'll see you again." He winked and walked through the courtyard, away from the castle.

Cade had something that Raith wanted. This could be fun.

Scarlett approached Cade wearily.

"Don't let Raith scare you." Cade reached his hand out and grabbed Scarlett's. "Better stick close to me, though. He likes to ruin anything that's mine."

The battle practice left Cade hungry. He tasted Scarlett, but her emotion level was still near empty. She should have stayed in her room and slept. What made her wander off?

His mother was right. Scarlett was crucial to his training. After he'd felt her emotion, an average human would seem meager. He'd better be more careful from now on. He needed to keep Scarlett—and to himself.

❧

Somehow, Scarlett had fought through the fog enough to try to leave. Whenever she was around Cade, she couldn't think clearly. Her mind had battled against his manipulation, but her way home was snatched from the grasp of her fingers. Raith was going to take her, she could feel it. Cade and Raith didn't get along. That was apparent from the glare Cade gave Raith when he saw Scarlett with him. She didn't know who he was at that point, but she hoped Raith would grab her and make her disappear before Cade called her. Instead, Cade took her back to her room where she'd spent the last three days.

Eventually, she would find a way home.

Cade entered her room. He had placed a spell on the door to keep Scarlett inside. Stupid magic. It always looked so wonderful in movies. In her life, not so much. Every time Cade came to the room, he drained her pain. She grew numb, until nothing mattered. He'd then kiss her and hold her close, until all she could think about were his hands on her body.

Then he'd leave.

No matter how determined she was to take control of the situation as she waited for his return, it always happened the same. As if someone else had hold of her whenever she was with him. She'd grow so dazed that escaping him no longer seemed important.

Most guys didn't leave until you slept with them. Not that Scarlett would know. She might not have been as innocent as her sister Ashleigh, but, somehow, she made it through high school without having sex. Not that people would actually believe her if she told them. Too many guys she dated told other stories, and she never cared enough to argue. She'd done plenty of other things to them, so there was no point in pretending she was an angel.

She hungered for the touch of someone else. Of a boyfriend twisting his hands through her hair, or down the curve of her hips. Finding a boyfriend was never hard. They flocked to her like magnets to metal. She was pretty, sure, but so were a lot of other girls. She had something else they didn't. She'd dated more guys than she cared to remember. But once the butterflies disappeared and they got bored of her saying no to sex, she'd dump them. The only guy she actually liked was Teddy, and she messed that up before it even began.

Scarlett hid under the covers, still in her nightgown. If she was stuck in this room, why bother putting on actual clothes? Cade sat on the bed next to her and pulled her blankets back. "As beautiful as you look in the nightgown, I think it's time you change into actual clothes."

"What's the point?" Scarlett asked.

After Cade drained her, she would lie on the bed, numb, for a few hours. But soon enough, her pain would return and so would her mind. She'd remember that she was stuck here, and that somehow she needed to get home. But when his lips were on hers, home was the last thing on her mind.

"I'm sorry I've kept you up here. Faerie is a dangerous place for humans." Cade rested his hand on hers. "I'll take you out and show you our world. I promise. First, though, we need to get you ready." Cade grinned. Scarlett couldn't deny he was beautiful. Inhumanly beautiful. Dangerously beautiful. Scarlett had let not-so-beautiful boys do all kinds of things to her. How was she going to resist Cade?

Peony was back to help Scarlett get ready. Apparently, Scarlett was to be Cade's date to a feast. He had been bringing her food to the room, but she'd only eaten half of it. It was her way of protesting being stuck, but all it did was leave her hungry. What she did eat was delicious. Warm turkey, or what tasted like turkey, with gravy and purple potatoes. Scarlett wondered what there would be to eat at a royal feast.

After a bath, Peony brushed Scarlett's hair and painted her face with make-up. Unlike last time when she used neutral colors, this time Peony applied a teal shadow to Scarlett's eyelids. She lined them with dark liner, then brushed mascara on her eyelashes. After some blush and lip gloss, Scarlett's makeup was done. Next was her dress.

"As Cade's human, all eyes will be on you," Peony said as she pulled a dress out of a garment bag. "The royal designer created this just for you."

The pale pink fabric shimmered from the light of the chandelier. The dress hugged Scarlett's bust, hips, and thighs and flared out at the bottom. The neckline dipped into a deep V and flaunted her cleavage. Scarlett felt like a walking mermaid. She sat on the bed while Peony curled her hair into long waves. The curling iron she used looked like Scarlett's back home, except there was no cord attached to it.

"Doesn't it need power?" Scarlett asked.

"It's powered with magic."

Oh, of course it was. Duh. What else would she expect? After Scarlett's hair was curled, Peony twisted a strand on each side and pinned them back. "Perfect."

Scarlett looked at herself in the mirror. She had thought she'd looked good when she went to senior prom.

Now, she actually looked like a princess. "Isn't it a little weird Cade is bringing a human to this feast?"

Peony fluffed Scarlett's hair with her fingers. "Yes, normally humans aren't as publicly paraded."

"Oh, and this feast, it's a big deal?"

"Cade and his brother Raith will be battling for the right to the throne at the end of the summer. This feast is the first event of the tradition."

"How do you know all this?" Scarlett didn't want to seem rude, but Peony was a human, too, and she seemed to know so much.

"I listen. You should, too."

Cade returned dressed in a gray suit with gold and maroon accents embroidered on the chest. He held silver fabric in his hand, which he handed to Scarlett. "To keep you warm."

Scarlett unfolded it to reveal a long, silky cape. She swung it over her shoulders. Cade buttoned the front for her. He latched his arm with hers and escorted her out of his room. They walked down the hall and to a wide set of stairs, which led down and opened into a large banquet room filled with long tables. Scarlett peered across the room, which was surrounded by balconies filled with tables that looked down upon them. A thousand eyes stared at Scarlett as she walked next to Cade. Kassandra sat at the head of the table text to a man wearing a crown. The king. Cade hadn't mentioned his father, but whatever Scarlett was expecting, it wasn't an old man with gray hair that sat upon his shoulders. The king's eyes drooped as he looked at Scarlett.

"Father," Cade said as he pulled out a chair for Scarlett. "This is Scarlett." He removed Scarlett's cape and laid it over her chair.

"A human?" the king said. He stared at her with a tilted head. Scarlett held her breath. What if he disapproved? "Welcome, Miss Scarlett. It's a pleasure to have you."

Scarlett sat down. Gold glassware had been placed in front of her. Chatter flowed through the room. Their table spread from one end of the room to the other, in between a similar table on each side. Above, guests looked down at them. "There are so many people here," Scarlett whispered to Cade.

"It's a celebration. I've challenged my brother to a battle at the end of the summer. This is the opening ceremony."

Peony had already told Scarlett this, but Scarlett didn't mention it. She didn't want Peony to get in trouble. A hush spread throughout the room. Scarlett followed everyone's stares to see Raith waltz into the room with a dark haired fae at his side. "Father, Kassandra." He bowed to them. "Cade, Scarlett." He winked at her. He didn't bother to introduce his date.

After everyone had taken their places at the table, the king stood. He pressed his fingers to the side of his throat and spoke, "Welcome. We've joined today to begin a summer full of festivities." His voice boomed through the room. He balanced himself with a cane in his left hand. "My youngest son Cade has challenged his brother Raith to the Right of Heir, which will take place on end of

Summer's eve. I wish them both well." The king reached his hand out. A wine glass, already full with a deep red liquid, flew to his hands. The king raised it, his hands shaking. "To my sons."

The room followed by raising glasses into the air and clinking them against one another. Scarlett joined in. She sipped the drink. It was fruitier than she was expecting. Every time she had wine, it was bitter and caused her to grimace. This was delicious. She drank some more.

"Fae wine is delicious," Raith said to Scarlett as he took a drink. "Quite lethal to humans."

Scarlett froze. Had this all been a trick? Did she just drink poison?

Cade reached his hand under the table and rested it on Scarlett's thigh. "Don't listen to my *brother*. Fae wine won't hurt you. It's just more potent than human alcohol, so you may want to take it slow."

"Or if you're spending the night with Cade, you may want to chug it." Raith raised his glass to Scarlett.

She swallowed a chuckle.

Women dressed in cherry red dresses with white aprons brought out dinner. Scarlett was pretty sure they were human. Slices of turkey and ham were placed on Scarlett's plate, paired with potatoes and a dish of fruit. Scarlett tried a piece that looked like pineapple, only it was blue instead of yellow. Like the wine, it was sweeter than she expected.

"So, brother, where did you meet such a lovely human?" Raith asked.

Cade sipped his wine. "It doesn't concern you."

"Curiosity has the better of me."

Scarlett looked away. It seemed awkward to be talked about like she wasn't there. She watched the humans walk around and fill the wine glasses from golden pitchers.

"That's fine with me," Cade said. He ran his hand up and down her leg, sending a shiver through Scarlett.

A woman approached their table. She lifted Kassandra's wine glass and poured more in. As she set it down, her hand slipped and knocked the glass over. Red liquid poured onto Kassandra's lap.

A rush of panic spread through Scarlett. Panic that wasn't her own. She could feel the woman's terror pulse through her veins as if *she* were the one the queen was glaring at. Scarlett closed her eyes and breathed in the surge of emotion, causing something to buzz inside of her. Iciness spread through her, like when she'd entered Faerie.

What was happening to her?

It had to be the wine. Whenever she hand drunk alcohol in the mortal world, a warmth would spread through her. This must have been the effect of the fae wine combined with spending so much time locked in a room, her mind now playing tricks on her.

"I'm so sorry, my queen," the woman stammered. "I will clean it up."

The queen stared at the woman. She huffed and flicked her hand. The liquid from her lap rushed back into the cup, which sat back on the table as if nothing had happened. "You are dismissed for the night."

The woman nodded and rushed away, taking her nervousness with her.

As the dinner finished up, people came over to congratulate Cade and Raith. Scarlett wasn't sure a battle against your brother really deserved congratulations, but, then again, she didn't know much about the Summer Court. The other fae at the dinner were all beautiful. Some had dark skin, others light, with hair ranging from blonde to midnight black. Most who approached glanced at Scarlett, but no one acknowledged her unless Cade introduced them.

A blonde woman eyed her as she reached Cade.

"Such a lovely dinner, my king and queen," the girl bowed. She was the only woman in the room not in a dress. Instead, she wore leather pants and vest. "Cade." She bowed again.

"Poppy, this is Scarlett." Cade gestured to Scarlett. "Scarlett, this is Poppy, my trainer."

Interesting. Poppy had an intensity in her eyes that made her look like she was ready to kick ass. She nodded to Scarlett, then turned her attention back to Cade. "I'd like to arrange next week's practice times, if you have a moment."

"Of course," Cade said as he stood. "I'll meet you at the top of the stairs, Scarlett. I think it's time we leave."

When Cade left with Poppy, Scarlett excused herself from the table and headed to the stairs. Someone followed.

"We meet again," Raith said as he caught up with Scarlett.

"I guess we do," she said.

He circled in front of her, blocking her path. "There's something different about you."

"Oh?" Scarlett would have thought he was crazy earlier, but after feeling the woman's emotion surge through her, she wondered if she was different. Had coming to a land of magic somehow changed her? Since following Cade through the door in the forest, her emotions felt like a roller coaster. One moment, she'd be full of pain. The next, numb. When Cade's mouth was on hers, lust filled her. Could the whirlwind of feelings make her crazy? Or had she really sensed the woman's anxiety? "Shouldn't you be with your date?"

"She'll survive." Raith tilted his head as he eyed Scarlett up and down. "My brother seems infatuated with you."

She tried to back away. Something told her Raith wanted nothing more than to hurt his brother and she had no desire to be a pawn in their chess game. "Not really."

"Your emotion is lovely. Right now, you're afraid I'm going to hurt you."

"Should I be?"

"Not of me," Raith said.

Scarlett turned and hurried up the stairs. She wasn't sure where she was going. All she wanted was to get home.

AFTER CADE SPOKE to Poppy about training, he went to the top of the stairs to find Scarlett. She wasn't there.

Instead, Raith sat on the top stair with his elbow resting on his knee, boredom on his face.

"Where's Scarlett?"

"She went that way." Gaze forward, Raith pointed behind him up the staircase.

"Leave her alone," Cade said. "She's mine."

"Quite the protective one, are we? And of a human."

"You only want her because I'm the one who found her." Cade marched up the staircase, stopping in front of Raith. "I need energy to train for our battle, and bringing a human here was easier than going to the human realm." He didn't need to explain himself to his brother. He didn't ask Raith how he replenished his magic.

"Then why not find a different human?"

Why did Raith care so much how Cade fed? Whatever the reason, Cade liked it. Scarlett was his, not Raith's.

Soon, the crown would be Cade's, too.

Chapter Eleven

I t was the first time she'd been out of Cade's room and away from him in three days, and Scarlett finally had a chance to run free. She wasn't sure what her plan was. She was in another realm, more than just a cab ride away from home. Unless there were realm jumping cabs here. Somehow, she doubted it. If she could get away from the castle, she could hide until she found someone to help her home. Not the greatest plan, but a plan nonetheless. It beat playing Rapunzel in the room Cade had trapped her in.

Her moments of clarity didn't last long. The mind fog she experienced after Cade numbed her pushed her desire to escape far away. This was her chance. She needed to act now before he could use his ability to control her emotions against her again.

Raith's words replayed in Scarlett's mind. *Not of me.* Maybe he was just trying to freak her out. Or maybe he was saying she should be afraid of Cade. Or Kassandra.

Something about the queen scared Scarlett. She'd always had good intuition about people, and her gut told her to steer clear of the Summer Queen. Maybe Scarlett had just read too many fairytales where queens were always evil, but if her intuition told her to be nervous, she would trust it.

Scarlett peered through a cracked door. She entered a library. Bookshelves lined the walls, filled with books, from floor to ceiling. Darkness filled the room, which was lit only by the moonlight sneaking inside through the large window on the other side of the room. Scarlett hurried across and peered outside. She was on the second floor of the castle. The courtyard hung below.

How long did she have before Cade found her?

Scarlett tried to pry the window open. It didn't budge.

She closed her eyes and pictured the window lifting. The iciness returned, subtler this time. Her veins warmed, heating her from the inside out.

The window slid up.

Like magic.

That didn't make sense. Had someone else opened it? No one else was in the room. Was her mind playing tricks on her? The longer Cade played with her emotion, the less in control of herself she felt.

She didn't know how she it opened, but she didn't have enough time to stop and worry. Carefully, she climbed onto the windowsill. The ground was at least ten feet away. She didn't have time to be afraid. She spun so her back faced the courtyard and then eased her body down as far as she could while hanging on. Then she dropped.

Scarlett's legs hit the ground with a thud. She fell backwards and landed on her butt. She'd be sore tomorrow, but she was out. Her dress constricted her movement, so she tore a rip in each side. She prayed no one would see her as she jogged through the courtyard. The moon and stars lit the night. They looked the same as if she were back home, lying on a blanket in the grass next to her mom and peering into the sky like they used to. Scarlett felt the pain creeping back in but pushed it away. She needed to focus if she wanted to escape.

On the far side of the courtyard, was a gate, a towering forest behind it. If she could make it there, she'd be harder to find. She ran faster. The gate was cracked open. Score. Scarlett hurried through it and into the cover of trees.

Now where?

She followed the path that led from gate. The forest was much darker. The trees were thick and kept the light out. Why couldn't she have escaped during the day? Her pace slowed as she gingerly stepped on the ground, careful not to turn her ankle.

Something shuffled in the trees.

"Who's there?" Scarlett asked. Walking alone down the street at home was scary enough. Being alone in a dark forest in a whole other world was much worse. Her desperation to leave had clouded her judgment.

A figure stepped out. A woman with nearly translucent

skin swayed toward Scarlett. "What a divine gift to find its way to me."

"Stay away," Scarlett said. She bent her legs and raised her fists.

"And what fear I feel." She cocked her head to the side and grinned. Her incisors were the longest of her teeth, like a vampire.

"What are you?" Maybe Scarlett could stall. Cade must be looking for her. So much for wanting to escape. But going back with Cade was better than whatever this lady wanted with her. "What do you want?" She tried to speak louder so someone might hear.

"Food as delectable as you is hard to come by in these woods."

"They'll know I'm missing. They'll come for you." Scarlett's heart pounded in her chest. Her mother's face flashed in her mind—not the lifeless face Scarlett had last seen, but a joy-filled face of love. She swallowed the terror immobilizing her.

The woman circled around her, hunger in her dark eyes. "I'll be long gone, and you'll be nowhere to be found."

Scarlett tried to think of something to do. Somewhere she could run. Something she could say to stop her. Instead, she froze.

The woman attacked.

THANK god the feast was over. Raith had a long summer

ahead of him. He preferred to be alone in his tree. If he had to be around other people, he'd choose people away from the castle. Court was boring. A whole world existed outside the castle walls, one free of ritual and expectation.

He walked through the courtyard to his door, which, to his surprise, he could see. Normally when he shut it, it glamoured itself invisible to anyone but him. When he got closer, he realized it was cracked open.

He heard voices. Strange. Most of the forest fae kept away from the castle, and most of the Summer Court kept even further away from the forest.

A scream made Raith move faster.

He sprinted through the gate and into the thicket of the forest. Another scream steered him on a path leading deeper into the woods.

A large figure pinned Scarlett's hands behind her back. She must have wandered out into the forest to get away from Cade. Maybe Cade should have warned her what would happen if she left the safety of the castle. Now she'd be eaten by a banshee. Too bad, too; she might have made the summer more interesting.

Raith could save her. He really *should* save her. A poor human seduced into a dangerous world. Here was Raith's chance to be a hero. The good guy. The misunderstood brother.

Terror pulsed from Scarlett. Raith breathed it in. Magic buzzed inside him.

Sympathy for the human filled him. too.

"Stop," Scarlett screeched.

"You smell so warm," the banshee said. She slid Scarlett's hair from her neck. "Ow," she said as she dropped her grip on Scarlett's wrists. "You burned me."

Scarlett lunged from her as she held her hands in the air. The banshee was too quick, though, and snatched Scarlett's leg and pulled her toward her. She lifted Scarlett by the ankle and sunk her teeth into her calf. Scarlett yelped and tried to break free, but she couldn't. Whatever she'd been able to do before didn't help her now.

Raith sighed. He'd helped a human once before. Out of pity, out of weakness, he wasn't sure, and he was about to help another one. He darted from the cover of the trees and slammed his body into the banshee. The banshee screeched as she released her grip on Scarlett and rolled into a crouch, anchoring herself between Scarlett and Raith. She hissed.

"She's mine now. It's too late for her."

Banshee venom was lethal to humans. It would kill them without the antidote, which Raith didn't have. He could just leave her to the banshee—pretend he was never here. But if he saved her, at least she wouldn't be eaten limb by limb, a less merciful death.

Raith pulled a knife from his boot and chucked it at the banshee. It hit her in shoulder. The banshee gasped, but she pulled it out and threw it back at Raith. Raith dove out of the way and landed with a summersault. The banshee pounced. She gripped his throat. Raith kicked her ten feet back. He hadn't filled his magic since yesterday. He hadn't expected a fight. A nice dinner, some banter, but not a banshee at his throat. The pain he'd absorbed from Scarlett was a start, but banshees were relentless. He needed more.

With his eyes closed, he breathed in the forest around him. He didn't have much time before the banshee would return. Magic entered his fingertips and moved through his hands. He pushed his palms forward. A murder of ravens flew from them. They pecked the banshee's eyes as she wailed.

Raith dusted himself off as he got up. The ravens struck until they faded away. The banshee clawed at her face. She would heal eventually—if nothing ate her first. But if he let her live, she might stick around for revenge. Banshees were spiteful like that. Annoyingly so. Raith brought his knife soaring to his fingers, and then he stabbed the pitiful creature in the heart, leaving it for something else to find as dinner.

Scarlett was curled into a ball on the cold forest floor. Blood dripped from the wound on her calf. Raith picked her up gently. She groaned but didn't stir. Once they were in his tree, he carefully placed her on the bed where she should be safe. He needed to go to the healing wing of the castle. Without medicine, Scarlett would die.

RAITH SLAMMED the gate as he returned. The antidote for banshee venom was gone. A fae wouldn't die from a bite, but it could get infected for a while without treatment. Apparently, a couple of banshees had moved closer to the castle and had been feeding off of unsuspecting fae. The healers were set to search the forest for the herbs needed to make more tomorrow, but it would be too late for Scarlett then.

He snuck into his tree. If Scarlett was still asleep, he didn't want to wake her. Then, if he didn't want to be a jerk, he'd have to tell her she would die. To his surprise, when he glanced at the bed, she was sitting up, looking at her leg.

"Bad night," Raith said.

Scarlett's neck snapped toward him. "Oh, it's you."

She wasn't afraid of him. That was good.

"What happened to me?" she asked. Her dress, now covered in dirt and leaves, had been ripped on each side, the slits sliced seductively high up her leg.

"When I showed up, you were fighting a banshee."

"Oh. That's what that thing's called?"

Raith didn't remind her that she had burned the banshee. That was unusual. Raith wasn't sure what it meant. When he checked her wound, he was surprised. It should have turned purple and started to spread already. Instead, it looked as if it were healing. He wet a cloth and wiped off the dried blood. All that was left was two bite marks. Somehow, Scarlett's body was repairing.

"Will I be okay?" She rubbed the wound.

"I think so," Raith said. He could tell her how unusual it was for her to still be alive. That even a Summer fae would be more affected by a bite than she seemed to be.

But he kept it to himself.

HEAT SOAKED into Scarlett's face. She remembered trying to leave the castle, the creature sinking its teeth into her leg and the searing pain that followed. Then everything went blank. Whatever happened next, she couldn't remember.

"You're awake," Cade said.

She must not have gotten very far.

"How'd I get here?" Scarlett asked as she opened her eyes. Cade sat on the edge of the bed. She was back in her room in the castle. So much for getting away. Night had come and gone and so had her chance to escape.

"You must have wandered off for a while. I found you in your bed with a ripped dress and dirt all over you."

Scarlett pushed herself up and leaned against the backboard. Her body was sore and her head hurt a little, but she felt mostly normal. Somehow she'd survived the attack and made it back inside the castle. If Cade hadn't helped her, who had?

"I have to go to battle practice, but when I get back, I want to show you around the grounds," Cade said. "I'm not going to lock you in. But I hope you'll wait for me."

After he left, Scarlett peeked out the door. She wanted to check if he was telling the truth, and it seemed he was. Her last escape attempt was an epic fail, so, for now, she'd stay put. If she got herself killed, she'd never make it home. While she waited, she decided to clean herself up. Whatever she'd done last night had left her caked in dirt.

Someone had to have brought her to Cade's room. Had she passed out? And what happened to that thing that attacked her? It had wanted to eat her. Scarlett was thankful it didn't.

She went to the bathroom and drew herself a bath. Her excursion had left her skin and hair dirty. When she dipped her feet into the claw foot tub, the temperature was perfect. She let her whole body sink into the hot water. The warmth relaxed her. After rinsing off of hair, she lifted her left leg.

On her calf, two round punctures swelled her skin.

Those were definitely new.

What else had happened last night, and why couldn't she remember?

Chapter Twelve

Scarlett had bathed and dressed in one of the gowns Cade had put in her closet. Not as fancy as the dress she had ruined last night, this one was various shades of green, its top tied together with a forest green ribbon. Scarlett would find a way home; she was determined. But in the meantime, this world made her curious. The magic, the ritual. The fact that she actually felt the emotion of someone course through her. She wanted to ask Cade if that was normal for a human, but she was pretty sure it wasn't, and that it meant something she didn't want Cade to know.

Or perhaps she simply wanted it to mean something else. She'd always felt out of place in life. Now, after losing her mother and fighting with her sister, she wanted nothing more than to belong somewhere. Could her mind be playing tricks on her in a pathetic attempt to convince herself she was more than a forlorn mortal who'd run away like a big, fat chicken?

Cade kissed her fingers before he took her arm in his hand and they began their day out of his room. Their first stop was at the top of one of the corner towers. A guard stood in front of the door, but he let Cade and Scarlett through.

Inside, weapons covered the walls of the round room.

"This is where I train." Cade let Scarlett look around the room.

Most weapons she recognized. Swords, staffs, daggers, a huge bow and arrow. Not that she'd ever seen any in person. "Can I touch them?"

Cade nodded.

Scarlett took a staff from the wall. It was wooden and light. She twirled it through the air. She wasn't sure how much good it would do against a metal sword that could chop it in half with one slice, but it felt less intimidating in her hands than a big sword.

Some of the weapons looked like the ones she'd seen on television. Some looked fancier, though, decorated with silver jewels. "Why do some have these?" Scarlett pointed to the jewel on the sword. It looked like a mini crystal ball.

Cade grabbed the sword by the handle and the orb's color glowed aqua. "Fae magic makes it faster and more powerful."

As Cade played around with the sword, Scarlett gripped the handle of a dagger. As her skin contacted the cold metal, its orb flickered violet. She released it, dropping it to the ground with a banging sound, and stepped away. It shouldn't have changed colors. She didn't have magic.

Or did she?

Cade picked up the dagger for Scarlett and put it back on the wall. "Wouldn't want you to hurt yourself." As he laughed, his eyes squinted. Sometimes Cade looked like a Norse god or an angel, but, every once in a while, he looked nearly human. A gorgeous human, of course. That's what made him so dangerous. He could put on a pair of jeans and a band t-shirt and have a whole sorority swooning over him at a frat party. He wouldn't even need to use any of his fae power. But if he did, no girl had a chance. He could make Scarlett forget her own name when he kissed her neck.

Why did Scarlett melt so easily to Cade's will? Was she just weak? Or was his fae-ability too strong for her to fight against?

AFTER THE TRAINING ROOM, Cade took Scarlett to the courtyard. When Scarlett was there last night, it was dark and empty. Everyone was enjoying themselves elsewhere after the feast. Today, people strolled through hedgerows and around bushes. Women dressed in gowns. Little girls and boys running around. On the far side of the courtyard was a market. They passed through the tents. There was a store that sold fruit that Scarlett had never seen before, one that sold wooden toys shaped as unrecognizable animals, another with swords, daggers, staffs, and other weapons. Cade stopped at a store with clothing and accessories. He grabbed a headband made of tiny lilac colored flowers Scarlett had never seen before.

A silver haired woman dressed in a gray dress that was torn at the bottom sat in the corner of the tent. "Only nine silver coins for a handsome man like you," she said. She must not know who he was. Scarlett wondered how many fae had never even met the people who lived in the castle. In the human world, everyone knew who the president was but he didn't know most of them. In a world without television, people probably never saw the royals.

Cade tossed her a gold coin. "Keep the change." He put the headband on Scarlett's head like a crown. She felt like a hippy. All she needed now was some weed and a peace-and-love attitude. Cade grabbed her hand and tugged her along. When their fingers touched, she felt a surge of emotion hit her like when the servant spilled the drink on Kassandra. Nervousness swirled with determination, topped with lust. Were those Cade's feelings or her own?

Something was happening to her, she just wasn't sure what.

They meandered through more of the shops. No one seemed to recognize Cade. A lot of girls stared at him, but no one treated him like he was fae royalty. People eyed her as if she were a black cat there to bring them a thousand years of bad luck.

Scarlett wanted to think it was because she looked so awesome in her dress and flower-crown, but she was pretty sure it was because she was human and was waltzing around hand in hand with Mr. Gorgeous. All the fae around had a certain beauty, an inhuman quality to their skin, hair, and eyes. Scarlett was flawed by comparison, but she was the one with Cade, not them.

"How come no one recognizes you?" Scarlett asked as they neared the end of the shops.

"I've glamoured myself to look different," Cade said. "To them, I look like someone who might work at the blacksmith's shop. Just an average Summer Fae."

"Then why are they all staring?"

"Ahh, because they sense you're human."

Just as she suspected. Only, she wasn't sure she *was* human. At least not a normal one, or else the orb on the sword wouldn't have changed color when she touched it. But Cade could be wrong. Surely, it was some weird coincidence. Scarlett was just looking into things too much.

Did she hope she was something more than human? Or would it make her life even more complicated than it already was? The idea of magic excited her. How many times had she wished for the ability to make the remote fly through the air to her when it was across the room? But even more importantly than that, she used to wish she had the ability to heal her mom's sickness.

As a kid, every year she wrote Santa a letter asking for a special pill to make her mom better. And every year, she was disappointed. Did the fae have the ability to heal humans?

Once they had visited all the shops, they turned back and walked down the street toward the palace. A group of fae women watched Scarlett, their bright eyes scanning her up and down. Scarlett linked her arm with Cade's and pulled him closer so they'd really have something to stare at.

Her mood was surprisingly good today. She couldn't remember the last time she felt this alive. She thought of home—of her mom, Ashleigh, her friends. Pressure built in her chest, threatening to burst. Then slowly, as if being syphoned out, the heaviness dulled and her cheerfulness returned.

Scarlett took in the world around her. The bright colors of the fae clothing, the rich azure color of the sky above—much deeper than the sky in the human world. Even the weather was perfect, the temperature pleasantly warm with the softest of breezes. Like a dream world. Why rush home? She was happy here, much happier than she'd been in such a long time. For once, the only person she needed to worry about was herself. For as long as Scarlett could remember, she'd felt like a parent to an unruly child. Her mom tried to mother her, and at times —when she was on her medication—things were great. But the cycle always continued. Her mom felt great. She didn't need her pills. Normal people didn't take something that altered their mind and her mom was normal.

When Scarlett tried to remind her that she felt good *because* of the pills, her mom would freak out, throwing things across the room, threatening to kill herself— because that was *totally* normal behavior.

And off the pills, things were worse.

She wasn't fooling herself. Cade wanted her for what her emotion could do for him. So what? She wasn't here to fall in love with a prince. But if he could keep her from the pressure she'd felt in her chest every day since her mom died, was it really so bad?

As they approached the castle, the guards eyed them. Cade nodded. The gates opened. He must have removed his glamour.

"Could someone use their glamour to pretend to be you?" Scarlett asked.

"Yes, but our guards have a gift that allows them to see through glamours."

Scarlett stored the tidbit away with everything else she'd learned so far. She'd taken Peony's advice to heart. Even if she'd decided to enjoy her time here, she needed to be prepared for whatever came her way. The more she could learn, the better.

Rather than going inside, Cade led Scarlett around the castle. Along the fence that surrounded the grounds, Scarlett looked for the gate she went through the night before but it was nowhere to be seen. Had she dreamed it?

Last night, she hadn't noticed all the roses that hedged the outside of the courtyard. She admired the flowers as they passed—the tips of the buds faded into a new color. Fuchsia roses turned orange on the ends, red to violet, yellow to white. After a bit of a walk, they made it to the back of the castle.

The fence continued around, trees towering on the other side. Why had Cade brought her here? There was nothing to see but grass. Then an iron gate appeared in the fence.

"How…" Scarlett asked as Cade, arm still linked with hers, led them through the gate.

Chapter Thirteen

Cade couldn't help but chuckle as surprise covered Scarlett's face. He inhaled the fresh smell of the salty sea. The boom of waves crashing roared as he and Scarlett left the shadow of the tress. The sand sank beneath their feet. As quickly as footprints had formed under each step, they disappeared with the next.

Since Scarlett's trip outside with Raith, Cade worried she might demand to be taken home. With his father's rule —fae weren't allowed to keep mortals against their will— he'd have no choice but to obey her request. She could ask if he'd take her home a million times and he didn't have to, but if she stated that he must take her home, he'd have no choice. He could keep threatening her with the pain she felt, but maybe a different approach would be better. The fae world offered many luxuries, and, as a prince, he could give her almost anything. Much more pleasant than the alternatives. So here Cade was, showing her all Faerie had to offer.

But he made no mistake; he would do whatever it took to keep her.

"You have an ocean here?" Scarlett watched as waves rolled onto the shore. "That's crazy!"

Cade thought of a blanket from inside the castle and it appeared in front of them, spread out across the sand. He unlinked his arm from Scarlett and sat on the blanket. Scarlett removed her shoes and floral headpiece, setting them next to Cade, and jogged toward the sea. She lifted her dress before her feet found the water.

Cade watched her spin as she laughed. She was stunning and not just for a human. A spark emanated from her —like a star in the night's sky, shining brightly, unaware of its innate allure. He'd been careful today when feeding from her emotion. He didn't want her fully detached. Instead, he wanted her to be free from the intensity of the pain but still herself. While he'd never admit it should anyone ask, he enjoyed the human's company. Unlike many of the fae women he'd spent time with, she wasn't obsessed with his position. Things would only get worse if he won the battle against his brother and became King of the Summer Court. Even now, as a prince, he was a prize to be had. The status of any woman he wedded and her family would rise upon marriage to a prince. But as the king's wife, she would become the second most powerful fae in the Summer Court.

Breathless, Scarlett plopped down beside Cade. "I've always loved the ocean."

"I can tell." Cade closed his eyes and felt the ocean breeze graze his skin.

"Don't you?"

"I do. As a child, my brother and I would sneak here and play in the waves. Mother would have thrown a fit if she knew, but we were careful. Once she caught us sneaking in, our pants soaked from the sea, but my brother thought quickly and told her we'd been playing in the courtyard fountain."

"Did she believe him?"

"Yes, but we still got punished, he more than I. Mother blamed his influence as my older brother. Apparently, I was too young to have such a devious plan."

"And now you have to battle him for the crown?" Her eyes were both curious and sad. He reached out his power and searched her for sadness. A small amount had surfaced inside her, but he left it alone.

"It's what I must do for my people."

"Raith wouldn't make a good king?"

"Mother doesn't think so."

"What about you?"

Cade wasn't sure what he thought. He thought of the brother who would always take the blame if they got caught somewhere they shouldn't be. The brother who helped Cade practice after their magic class as their magic was developing because Cade was having a hard time controlling his but didn't want to disappoint their father. He wasn't sure when things changed, but they did, and now Cade wasn't sure how Raith would rule.

"I don't think he really wants to be king," Cade said. "And I can't risk it. Not with the Summer Court at stake."

Scarlett rolled up the sleeves of her emerald dress and hiked up her skirt so her calves and lower thighs were warmed by the sun. Cade slipped off his boots and socks, but left his clothes as they were.

"Do you visit the sea much?" Cade asked.

"I used to, then life got busy." Scarlett's eyes were closed as she leaned back, propped up by her elbows. Her long, chocolate hair flowed behind her, waving slightly from the breeze. "Is this beach just for the Summer Court?"

"It borders both Summer and Spring. Faerie is an island, but the other courts are bordered by mountains."

"Is there a court for each season?"

"Yes, unfortunately." The Spring Court was tolerable, but Cade could do without the others. "The Autumn and Winter Courts can be...problematic."

"Oh?" Scarlett twisted to her side, now using her elbow to prop her head as she looked at Cade.

"Faerie used to be completely separate from the mortal realm, and, a very long time ago, there used to be only two Fae courts: the Seelie and the Unseelie. Eventually, the Unseelie King found the connection between realms and let his creatures go *exploring*. Needless to say, it wasn't good for humans. But some Seelie fae crossed realms and decided that humans needed protection. Not all the Seelie fae agreed. Many thought humans should fend for themselves, that it was beneath them to worry about mortals when their lives were barely a breath to us fae."

"How chivalrous." Scarlett huffed. "So, there were two and now there are four courts?"

"Six. Some of the Seelie and Unseelie fae preferred the human realm and so they built their courts amongst the mortals. They learned quickly that human emotion was especially potent. See, before the realms were connected, the fae fed off of the emotion of each other. Once they found the humans, that all changed. But the nobles of the Seelie and Unseelie courts were greedy and didn't want all the fae to stay in the human realm, so they each created two courts to remain in Faerie, each tied to the realm by a season."

"So, you can't leave Faerie?"

"We can, but if our allegiance belongs to one of the season courts, we must return to our court at the very least for our season."

"Your season?"

"Like in the human world, the seasons change here in Faerie. Each court has its chance to rejuvenate its power and be at its strongest."

"Do the human realm courts follow the seasons?"

"No, they are uninhibited in their power. When they left Faerie, they bound ours. Each court was given a strength and each individual one part of that strength."

"What do you mean?"

"We Summer fae were gifted the power of the mind. Each of us has our own unique form of the gift. I can enter dreams, Raith can see memories, some can see the future. Things like that."

Cade wasn't sure why he was telling her all of this. Perhaps it was the inquisitiveness that danced on her features, from her wide blue eyes to her parted peach lips. Or perhaps it was just a chance to talk to someone with genuine interest who cared to know about him and his life.

"But the Seelie and Unseelie Courts have all their power?" Scarlett sat up now and pulled her knees into her chest, her gaze ahead toward the waves.

"Cruel, huh." Cade smirked. "They bound us to the realm and limited our power, while they can go wherever they please, full magic."

"Do they get along?"

"God, no. They hate each other. But balance is required for the fae, and if one light court has full power, then one dark court must as well."

"Dark and light?"

"The Seelie Court is good while the Unseelie Court is not, at least relatively. All Fae are out for themselves, if you ask me."

Scarlett tilted her head toward Cade. "Even you?"

"Yes, for my people." He would do what needed to be done to protect his people, including suck the woman in front of him dry of emotion if needed. Which meant he'd already said too much to Scarlett. But he'd felt her pain in that graveyard, and even if she knew she was just a piece in his puzzle, Cade didn't think she could leave him.

"Come on, come in the water with me," Scarlett said. "Please." She pouted her lower lip.

How long had it been since he'd felt the ocean? Five, six years, maybe more? He looked at Scarlett's pleading look. Who knew the next time he'd get the chance to be free. If he won the battle, he'd be too busy with royal duties. And if he lost... Well, he may never have the chance again.

He rolled up his pants. "Only my feet."

"Yay!" Scarlett bounced up. She untied the green ribbons on the top of her dress then slipped the dress over her head, leaving her in her slip, her bra and panties peeking through the thin fabric. She reached out her hand and pulled Cade up, dragging him to the shore.

The water splashed against his ankles. Just as he remembered, the water felt pleasant against his skin, its temperature warm. As children, he and Raith would hurl their clothing off and sprint straight into the waves, no modesty between brothers.

Scarlett was in to her thighs now, not even bothering to hold up her slip.

"Be careful, the waves can become unpredictable," Cade said. Not only did the waves have a mind of their own, but creatures roamed their waters. They should be safe this close to the castle, though. The water fae knew better than to attack here.

She ignored his warning and waded further into the sea. She twirled, water waist high, glancing at him with joy gleaming from her face. Scarlet held her arms out wide and tilted her face toward the sun. But she leaned back too far and fell back into the waves.

Cade rushed to her, pushing easily through the water

with his fae strength. Before he reached her, her head surfaced. Scarlett laughed as she stood. "I knew that would get you in here."

"How conniving." Cade wrapped his arm around her waist and tugged her close.

Scarlett's hair, now wet, shined in the sunlight. "You're a fae prince. You need to have fun."

He lifted her, her face inches from his. Gently, Cade pressed his lips onto hers. "This is more fun than I've had in a long time."

They didn't kiss again. Cade didn't feed from her emotion. Once out of the water, he used his magic to dry them both. Scarlett glided the dress over her curves and tightened the ribbons across her chest. Her hair had dried, but still held its natural wave. She placed the flower head-band back across her forehead, and Cade swore—minus her rounded ears— she nearly looked fae.

After they were back in the courtyard, Cade made the gate vanish behind him. Only he and Raith could use it, and he doubted his brother even thought about the ocean any more.

Chapter Fourteen

C ade escorted Scarlett back to her room then excused himself to attend to royal duties.

He had dried her with his magic, but she still felt salty from the seawater. She removed her dress and slip and made her way to the tub. Scarlett turned the knobs and water poured out of the spout. She was glad to be able to tend to herself. Having someone wait on her made her feel like a princess, but it seemed wrong. Even if Peony had chosen to be here, Scarlett didn't need a servant.

Scarlett climbed into the tub as it filled. The warm water soaked into her skin, relaxing and loosening her tense muscles. She dipped her head under. When it resurfaced and she opened her eyes, her heart raced. Raith stood there, leaning against the wall.

"What do we have here?" he asked, eyebrows raised.

"Get out." Scarlett clenched her teeth.

Bubbles formed in the tub as the water turned off. "Better?"

At least her body wasn't on full display now. "Can I help you?"

"You make me curious."

"I'm glad."

"And you're spunky, too."

"You're welcome."

"I'm here to give you some advice."

Peony's warning played through Scarlett's mind—*I listen and you should, too.* The next time she decided to make an escape, she wanted to be more prepared. When Raith had found her in the courtyard, she'd sensed he might help her. Staying on his good side could be a smart decision.

"I'm listening."

He stepped away from the wall, staring at Scarlett with his bright blue eyes. "Be careful of my brother. He'll do anything to win the crown."

"And you won't?" His *I'm-only-here-to-warn-you* game didn't fool her.

"I didn't say you should trust me."

"Thanks for the warning."

He turned away from Scarlett. "And be careful where you explore alone from now on, lest you wind up something's lunch."

Then he vanished.

How'd he know about that creature?

Scarlett enjoyed the rest of her bath free of any more interruptions. She tried desperately to recall more about the night she'd tried to escape. Something had happened. Something she couldn't remember. Something Raith somehow knew about.

When she went to the bed to slip her dress back on, she found an orange tipped fuchsia rose lying across it.

Cade didn't return until the next morning, his mood so different than when they were together at the sea. It wasn't that he was in a bad mood, but he was stiff compared to the free-spirited moment they shared just the day before. After a night of bad dreams, Scarlett wasn't the girl at the sea anymore either. The pressure in her chest that had flared in her sleep eased minutes after Cade arrived.

He told her that Peony would be in that afternoon to help her prepare. Tonight was the opening ball to officially commence the challenge for the Right of Heir and he wanted Scarlett to be his date.

She wondered if it was strange for a potential future king to bring a mortal to such a big event, but she didn't voice her concerns. Scarlett spent most of the day reading a book she found on a shelf in her room. It was full of fae versions of fairytales, even darker than the ones the Grimm brothers wrote. She considered strolling out to the courtyard for some fresh air, careful this time and staying well within the castle boundaries, but decided to open a window instead. The last thing she wanted was to run into Raith again. She would see him soon enough at the ball tonight and be forced to listen to any more brilliant advice he had—if Cade allowed him to talk to her, that was.

Peony arrived as the sun dipped behind the forest, its

orange glow still lighting the sky. "Miss Scarlett." She curt-sied when she entered the room, a large garment bag in her hand.

Scarlett curtsied back. Earlier that morning, she'd spent an hour practicing. It seemed like an important skill in the fae world. Peony's eyes widened. "Should I draw you a bath?"

"I already took one."

"Then I will do your hair."

After Scarlett put on her slip, Peony curled Scarlett's hair into long, loose curls. She pinned a strand from each side back at the crown of her head and added a silver leaf headband. Then, Peony painted Scarlett's face with peach colors, light eye shadow and a glossy lip.

Scarlett followed Peony back to the bedroom. Once there, Peony opened the garment bag and pulled out a lavender dress. She held it up for Scarlett to see. The lacy top had a halter strap and heart shaped neckline. The skirt was chiffon and fell to the floor.

"It's gorgeous," was all Scarlett could manage to say. It was the prettiest dress she'd ever seen. Peony helped Scar-lett into the dress, buttoning the long trail of buttons on the back. Scarlett took herself in as she glanced in the mirror. The dress's silver belt cinched at her waist, matching the leaf headband, which sat perfectly like a crown on her head.

"You look lovely." Cade stood in the doorway, in a deep brown coat with embroidered silver swirls paired with brown leather pants and boots. "Are you ready?"

Chapter Fifteen

C ade twined his arm with Scarlett and led her down the hallway. She felt good this evening, no twinge of pain creeping in. Were things getting easier? Or was Cade to thank? They walked down a set of stairs and through another hallway before arriving at the grandest staircase Scarlett had ever seen. The wide stairs with dark wood railing led halfway down the flight before curving the other way. Columns accented the top and bottom of the staircase. A male fae with mahogany hair, dressed in a suit, stood at the top of the stairs and nodded to Cade.

"Announcing Prince Cade and his human, Scarlett," the fae man said.

Cade's *human*? He didn't speak the word in a vile manner, but something felt off about it. But what did Scarlett expect? That she'd be announced as his date? She kind of did. Definitely not being thought of as his *human*.

There wasn't anything she could do about it now, so

she let Cade guide her down the staircase. Scarlett stepped carefully, fearful of tripping in the heels she wore. The room below was full of fae. All flawless and dressed elegantly. Scarlett could feel something buzzing in the room, an energy of sorts.

When they reached the bottom of the stairs, Cade led Scarlett to the side. The floor beneath her was a luxurious tile, a silver and fuchsia pattern spread throughout the room. They stood next to Kassandra and the king, who stared blankly ahead as if his mind was off in some distant land. Scarlett gave a small curtsy, which Kassandra returned.

"Announcing Prince Raith and his human, Natalie," the fae man's voice echoed through the room.

Natalie? As in her best friend's name? It must have just been a coincidence. Natalie was a popular enough name. Scarlett's gaze snapped to the top of the stairs. There, her best friend stood, arms linked with Raith's. She wore a crimson, floor length gown with an opaque lace neckline. Natalie's eyes doubled when she saw Scarlett. Her foot slipped on the stair and she tilted to the left. Raith's hand quickly moved to her waist and kept her close.

When they reached the bottom stair, Raith looked at Kassandra and the king. Scarlett swore she could feel anger radiating off Kassandra when she took in Natalie, but her expression didn't give any feeling away. Natalie kept her jaw clamped shut, her eyes wide with fear. Even her human instincts must sense the distaste pouring off of Kassandra.

"Let the dance begin," the fae at the top of the staircase said.

The crowd drifted to the outside of the room, creating an opening in the middle. Cade guided Scarlett inside and spun her to face him. He bowed. Scarlett wasn't sure what to do, so she curtsied. He nodded in approval. Then he pulled her close and they danced.

Piano music bounced through the room, but Scarlett didn't see a piano. The desire to play consumed her. How long had it been now? Too long. The song was a waltz. Scarlett's shoulders swayed to every third beat. With closed eyes, she envisioned her hands moving across keys to Chopin's Waltz in B Minor, her mother's favorite. Its sad melody sang in her head, blocking out the noise around her. A memory surfaced.

"Why do you always like the sad songs?" Scarlett asked her mom.

"There's a beauty to sadness," her mom replied.

Scarlett's fingers played Fur Elise. "And this isn't beautiful?"

"In its own way. But so overplayed." Her mom grinned. It had been a good week so far. No complaints as Scarlett watched her take her pill every morning, and, more importantly, no voices.

Scarlett jerked herself from the memory and tore her eyes open. She couldn't deal with her grief right then, not there in front of all those people.

Cade led Scarlett across the dance floor as Raith did the same with Natalie. Scarlett tried to keep her gaze on Cade, but she couldn't stop an occasional glance to her best friend. Why was she here? It couldn't possibly be a coincidence that Raith needed to bring a human to the ball and he chose Natalie. Had Cade told him about her? Scarlett doubted so. Any time she saw Raith and Cade converse, a smoke trail of animosity radiated from both of them. She doubted Raith would go to Cade for anything, especially not which human to select.

The crowd watched the two couples dance. When the first song was over, they stopped. Scarlett wondered if the crowd would join now, but no one moved. Cade's expression tightened, then Scarlett felt a hand on her shoulder.

"Hello, love," Raith purred. "Dance with me?"

Scarlett glared at him.

"Now, now." Raith slipped his hand around Scarlett's lower back. "Tradition is tradition."

Cade's eyes met Scarlett's. "We switch partners for *one* dance. Then you're mine again."

There it was again, the possessiveness. Raith pulled Scarlett away before she could respond, but not before a chill radiated through her bones. If she didn't discover a way to leave soon, she never would. Cade had as much as peed on her like a dog marking its favorite tree. But everything had grown more complicated now that Natalie had found her way to Faerie. Even if Scarlett found a way home, she couldn't leave her there.

"I'm a much better dancer than my brother. You should be thanking me." Raith grinned as he twirled her.

"Why her?" Scarlett asked.

"Your friend, Natalie? I thought you'd be grateful. A friend in such a strange place should be a comfort."

"This world is dangerous. She shouldn't be here."

"Ahh, but you're here."

"That's different."

Raith's hand moved lower, grazing just above Scarlett's butt. He pulled her closer. "You're not the only one trying to escape her demons."

Did he mean that Natalie was running from something, too? She was one of the happiest people Scarlett knew. The eternal optimist, the burst of sun on a gray-skied day.

"What do you mean?"

Raith's gaze met Scarlett's. "That's not my secret to tell. Just know she came here willingly."

Scarlett glanced at her best friend. She'd been so preoccupied with her own problems, when was the last time she asked Natalie how things were going? Scarlett would have noticed if something was wrong, though. Maybe. Or had she been too busy?

"After the ball, take her home," Scarlett said. "Please."

"Such polite manners. I bet those big blue eyes work wonders on the human boys at home."

"Quit patronizing me." Scarlett's eyebrows tightened. "I should have known you were just trying to be an ass."

Raith removed his hand from Scarlett's shoulder and placed it on his heart. "You wound me." He moved his fingers up to Scarlett's chin and lifted it so her eyes met his. "I didn't say no. We could work out a bargain."

Scarlett's heart flickered. If there were a way to save Natalie, she'd do it. "What kind of a bargain?"

"A fae bargain." Raith smirked. "If you haven't been warned, you should never make a bargain lightly."

"Why would you tell me that if it's you I'm bargaining with?"

Raith shrugged. "I'm in a good mood."

The song ended and Cade, arm linked with Natalie, headed toward them.

"Meet me here at three in the morning, and we'll sort out the terms," Raith said.

"You can't hurt her in the meantime. Or take advantage." Scarlett would do what it took to keep Natalie from being sucked into this world, but she needed to know that she would be okay until she could make the bargain with Raith.

"After the ball is over, I will keep my hands to myself. But she has to finish her duties as my date." Raith held out an empty hand. A pocket watch appeared in his palm. "Don't be late or I'll assume you've changed your mind."

Scarlett took the watch and stuffed it into the side of her dress underneath the cover of her arm. Raith backed away from her with a wink. "Natalie, dear, another dance?"

Natalie looked nervously at Scarlett. She must not have known that Scarlett was here. What made her agree to come in the first place? Sure, Raith was attractive. If you liked the cocky type. Did Natalie come just to see another world? Had Raith told her he was a fae prince? Or was he telling the truth when he said Natalie was fighting some demon, and, like Cade did with Scarlett, Raith took away her pain?

Scarlett grinned at Natalie. She couldn't find the right words to say, so she kept silent. But Natalie smiled back and Scarlett's shoulders relaxed. Neither knew why the other was there, but they were still friends. And even though Scarlett was determined to get Natalie home safely, Raith was right. Having a familiar face in the unfamiliar world was nice.

With the second dance over, the crowd joined in. The ballroom filled with dancing pairs, twirling across the dance floor in coordination like the gears of a clock.

"Come with me," Cade said. Scarlett followed him outside of the dancing, to the edge of the room. Plates of food and pitchers of wine filled the tables covered in cream-colored linens. "I have something to attend to. Help yourself to anything while I'm gone."

He headed back through the crowd. Scarlett was alone. At first, she stood awkwardly next to the refreshment tables like a loner at prom. She watched the couples glide across the room, smiles on their faces. Almost everyone was dancing now, at least from what Scarlett could see. Except for a tall, brown haired fae in the corner of the room who watched Scarlett. He wore a maroon jacket similar to Cade's. Scarlett had never seen him before. Why did he seem so interested in her? Probably because she was some lowly human here to please a prince. She turned back toward the refreshment table.

Her stomach grumbled. The fruit looked delicious. The strawberries' bright red color made Scarlett's mouth water.

"Fae food makes human food seem bland. Once you taste it, there's no going back," an unfamiliar male voice said from behind Scarlett. She didn't see anyone approach her. How did he get so close without her noticing?

She turned to see a tall fae, with wavy, chin length navy hair peering at her with steel eyes. His suit was more modern than the other fae here—like some Armani model.

"I've eaten fae food before."

"Then how are you resisting these delectable strawberries?" The fae took one from the silver platter and bit into it slowly, eyes locked with Scarlett's.

"If you're trying to be sexy you're utterly failing." A total lie. God, what made fae so attractive? Scarlett could see herself on top of him, riding him like a…

Stop it! Focus, Scarlett. Head out of the gutter. What had gotten into her?

He smirked as he chewed the strawberry. "Can't say I didn't try."

"Shouldn't you be out there dancing?" Scarlett broke eye contact with him and looked out into the crowd. Where did Raith and Natalie go? Should Scarlett try to find them?

"Worried about your friend?" The fae tossed another strawberry into his mouth.

"Excuse me?" How did he know who Natalie was?

"Your mind is an open book, darling."

Shit. Could he read her mind?

He nodded.

"Stop it!" What an asshole, peering into her thoughts without permission.

"I've been called worse."

Scarlett searched for Natalie again, wanting to look anywhere but into this fae's eyes. Something about him brought out the dirty side of her imagination. Almost as if it was out of her control.

Cade weaved through the dancing couples toward Scarlett. She sighed with relief. For once, spending time with him seemed the safest option.

"Well, hello there, *Prince* Cade," the fae said. He popped a grape into his mouth. "How rude you are to leave poor Scarlett here all by her lonesome."

"Kaelem," Cade said in vicious tone. "Who do I blame for your presence?"

"Your mother," Kaelem said. "She invited all the courts' monarchs, as tradition dictates."

"I'm surprised you fit us into your busy schedule." Cade pulled Scarlett close to his side, his arm lingering around her waist.

"And miss a brotherly duel? This time, I'll get to be a spectator. A pleasant change."

"Well, thank you for the interest, but Scarlett and I will be going back to the dance floor now."

"Ahh, yes, enjoy some dancing before the feeding."

Cade stiffened next to Scarlett.

"Does poor Scarlett not know what she signed up for? And you summer fae think you're *nice* to the mortals." Kaelem shook his head side to side.

"What feeding?" Scarlett asked. He hadn't mentioned she'd be attending the ball with him until today and he definitely didn't say anything about a *feeding*.

"It's a ritual to open the challenge ceremony," Kaelem

said. "The two brothers must feed off of the energy of the same sacrifice while she relives her darkest memory. But don't worry, dear Scarlett. It's only *one* of the dates. Some courts have the girls fight and loser is stuck with the honor. Others roll a die."

Why wouldn't Cade have warned Scarlett? Then again, what did she expect? She was *his* after all, or so he'd said over and over again. A mere hen led into a world of foxes, now wondering why they fought over her for breakfast.

"Oh, how rude of me," Kaelem said. "Sometimes it's a princess battling, not a prince, and she brings a male mortal as her date. Unless she's a lesbian, of course. Love is love."

"Come on, Scarlett." Cade looped their arms. "Let's dance." He pulled her away.

Scarlett looked back at Kaelem, both annoyed and thankful he'd warned her. He winked before Scarlett disappeared into the crowd.

Chapter Sixteen

Neither Scarlett or Cade spoke as he led her in a dance. The piano music was nothing more than a muffle in Scarlett's ear as she thought about the mess she'd gotten herself into. All because she was too weak to face her pain. Life with her mom hadn't raised her to be so delicate, but even the thought of her mother brought a clench to Scarlett's stomach. She felt the tenseness disappear.

"I want you to be happy," Cade said.

Of course he was feeding from her emotion. That's why he brought her here, after all. Scarlett didn't respond.

"Don't let Kaelem get to you. He's an ass." Cade's hand kept Scarlett's body close to his. "I didn't tell you about the ritual because I didn't want you to worry. It isn't so bad."

She saw the lie in his eyes and swore she felt guilt under his surface. "Who is he?"

"Kaelem? The newest king of the Unseelie Court. The power has gone to his head."

"You two have a history?"

Cade shrugged. "He's a year older than Raith, so we saw each other at occasional cross-court functions growing up. He's always been a cocky bastard, the Unseelie crown is just the icing on the cake."

The fae who announced everyone walked back up the stairs to a balcony overlooking the ballroom. "Attention everyone. It is now time for the opening ritual to begin."

Scarlett searched the room for Natalie and found her and Raith near the stairs. Natalie was laughing about something. Cade directed Scarlett toward them. Each couple walked up the stairs to the announcer.

"We begin the opening ritual of the Battle of Heirs. One human will be used, and as the oldest participant, Raith decides how to select the human."

"Rock paper scissors?" Raith replied.

"I'll do it," Scarlett blurted. She'd already known it should be her, and the words slipped out of her mouth before she could talk herself out of it. If it weren't for her, Natalie wouldn't be here. She was sure of it. If one of them had to face a past pain, it should be her.

The announcer looked to Raith, who quickly said, "Or that."

Scarlett pulled her arm away from Cade's. He glanced at her, eyebrows creased. If that was worry on his face, Scarlett didn't see the point. He knew she could be the one chosen for whatever this ritual was.

"Very well." The announcer pulled a small vial of

black liquid from his pocket. He popped off the lid. "Drink this."

Scarlett gripped the vial with her thumb and index finger and lifted it in front of her face. Energy buzzed from it. Who knew what it would do to her? But if she wouldn't drink it, then Natalie would have to. Before she could change her mind, Scarlett poured it down her throat.

The liquid was thick like tar but tasted like grape juice with a hint of mint. It wasn't bad, but it wasn't good either. As it slid down her esophagus, it grew warmer.

The announcer took the vial from her.

Cade and Raith each grabbed one of her hands.

The warmth grew hotter until Scarlett's insides burned. Her vision blurred. The world around her blackened. There was no sound or smell or feeling of any sort. Just darkness.

Then everything changed.

She was walking up to her house, alcohol on her breath. The party had been fun, and, to her relief, Teddy wasn't there. She'd missed him like crazy, but if she had to see him at a party with another girl again, she'd lose it.

Wait, Scarlett knew this moment. No, no, no. She tried to pull away from Cade and Raith—to make it stop. She couldn't relive this. Not like this. This felt too real. She'd had nightmares of it nearly every night, but they were different. This was as if her life was a movie and she was replaying the scene. The remote wasn't hers to control.

The night was dark, cloud cover blanketing the moon above. Scarlett fumbled for her keys in her purse, but her front door was cracked. Sweet. She pushed the door open quietly, careful not to wake her mom.

She didn't want to see this again.

Something smelled off—metallic. Scarlett switched the living room light on and her world shattered. Her mom was sprawled out in the middle of the room, long slits crawling up her wrists like snakes, lying in a pool of blood.

No. No, no, no.

Scarlett dropped her purse and rushed to her mom. She dropped to the ground, blood seeping into her clothes. Her fingers touched her mom's neck, searching desperately for a pulse. Nothing.

No.

Her mom's eyes stared blankly at the ceiling. Scarlett crawled to her purse, leaving a trail of blood behind her. She searched frantically for her phone and dialed 9-1-1.

When the paramedic told Scarlett her mom was gone, Scarlett's legs buckled as she fell to her knees.

The bomb inside Scarlett exploded. She couldn't feel her body anymore. The following hours blurred together. She didn't know anything except that her mom wasn't here anymore.

And, for a brief moment, a small part of Scarlett felt relieved.

She'd been avoiding that feeling since the moment it had hit her, desperate to forget she could have ever thought something so abhorrent. She was a horrible, horrible person. The worst. What kind of daughter feels alleviation when her mother kills herself?

The memory, if that was what it was, faded away and the ballroom appeared again. The pain inside Scarlett pulsated through her. She couldn't handle it. The nausea inside her grew.

Chapter Seventeen

R aith felt the misery inside Scarlett vibrate through her and into him through their latched hands. He knew Cade would be feeling it, too.

Something inside Raith changed. His power buzzed inside, threatening to burst right there. He continued to absorb the emotion Scarlett spewed. He had seen the vision that played through her mind—her darkest memory. He could feel her love for her mother and her heartbreak with her mother's last breath—and her guilt. He, too, knew the anguish of being motherless. But the feeling of betrayal that hit Scarlett when relief struck her was foreign to Raith. He'd missed his mother with every fiber of his being since the moment she'd died.

The power continued pouring into Raith until Scarlett collapsed. Both he and Cade kept their grip on her hands and gently lowered her to the ground.

The announcer spoke. "And so begins the Summer Court Battle of Heir."

The crowd cheered.

"What's wrong with her?" Raith asked the announcer.

"She's been drained. She'll recover." Could he sound any more apathetic? Scarlett's skin was nearly as pale as snow. The announcer could at least pretend to feel bad for the mortal.

"Don't worry about her," Cade said. "You have your own date."

Raith found Natalie a few feet away, gaping at her friend on the floor. He glanced back at Scarlett. Cade was right, Scarlett was his. For now. And Raith needed to keep Scarlett's friend calm.

"What did you do?" Natalie asked Raith as he approached her.

"The liquid she drank caused her to relive her worst memory," Raith told her. "And then when she felt the pain, we took the pain from her like I've done for you."

Natalie bit her lip. "Is she going to be all right?"

Raith nodded. "Cade will take care of her. She's too valuable for him to do otherwise. Come now, let's get out of here."

They would go back to his room, he'd give her some fae wine, and she'd fall asleep. Then he would see if Scarlett cared enough to save her.

⚜

BLACKNESS ENVELOPED SCARLETT. She jerked her eyes open and took in her surroundings. The familiar silk sheets sent relief through her. She wasn't in the nightmare world. Thank god.

But something felt wrong. That place was horrible, but she didn't feel agony inside anymore. She felt like all her cares had been pumped from her, leaving her weightless.

She was no longer in the dress she wore to the ball. Someone must have taken it off of her, leaving her in just her slip. Scarlett turned on her side. Moonlight poured through the window, dimly lighting the room. Something gold and shiny caught Scarlett's attention—a pocket watch. It meant something, but what?

Her eyes grew heavy. She was tired, so tired. They blinked, threatening to shut, but then the darkness would return. Scarlett stared at the watch, trying desperately to remember what it was for.

Someone had given it to her earlier—at the ball, maybe? Why was everything so fuzzy? Her arms tingled at her side. She was supposed to go somewhere at a certain time. That was it. Raith had given Scarlett the watch as they danced. She wanted something from him.

Think, Scarlett, think, she told herself.

The vision of her mother, cold on the ground, eyes blank, surfaced. No. Focus. Scarlett was supposed to meet Raith to make a bargain.

Why even bother to remember? Thinking felt too difficult—like moving hands through wet cement. It would be so much easier to fall back asleep.

No, her subconscious screamed at her. Whatever she was struggling to remember was important.

It was about the ball. Someone at the ball. Scarlett

remembered meeting the Unseelie King—Kaelem—and his cocky, gorgeous face. A smile threatened to surface on Scarlett's face, but the thought alone stole all of her energy.

Kaelem, not Cade, warned her about the ritual. And he could read her thoughts. He knew who Natalie was.

Natalie. She was here in this realm. And Raith said he'd make a bargain with Scarlett to send Natalie back if Scarlett met him at three in the morning.

Scarlett pushed herself up, her body stiff. What if she was too late? How long had she been asleep? The questions weren't going to help so she reached for the pocket watch and opened it. Two-fifty-seven. She would have to hurry, but she could make it.

She glanced down at her slip. There was no time to change. It covered her, mostly. Enough, at least. If she had to run down there naked to save Natalie she would— whatever it took. She may have been a crappy daughter, but Scarlett refused to be a bad friend.

With no shoes, she hurried down the hallway. No one else was in sight, the whole castle likely asleep after the ball. How long had they celebrated after Scarlett had been drained?

She kept her feet light on the floor, careful not to wake anyone. She didn't need Cade finding out about her late-night rendezvous. Her meeting Raith would not go over well, especially in so little clothing.

Then again, as much as Cade would like to believe otherwise, Scarlett was not his.

The ballroom seemed so huge from the top of the

stairs now that it was empty. Scarlett looked to the balcony where she drank that vile liquid.

But wait, the ballroom was empty, no Raith to be found. She checked the watch. Three o'clock sharp. She was here right on time. If that ass lied to her…

"I can feel the wrath radiating off of you like heat from a fire." Raith stepped out of the back-corner shadows.

"I figured you were an ass who stood me up."

"I could never stand you up, love."

She didn't have time for his fake flattery. Somehow, he knew Natalie was her friend so he preyed on her weakness to lure her here. Scarlett wouldn't be surprised if tricking her into a bargain was his plan all along.

"So, let's bargain." She walked down the stairs and met Raith in the middle of the room, which was lit by the moonlight shining through a huge skylight above. Scarlett hadn't noticed it during the ball. It was too busy then— too full of fae staring at her.

Now, Raith's eyes were the only ones watching her. "I'm glad you dressed comfortably. Wouldn't want to be overdressed for a bargain."

"Thanks to that stupid ritual, I was blacked out until a few minutes ago. You're lucky I woke up in time and showed up at all."

"No, *you're* lucky," Raith said. "You are the one who wants to save your friend."

"There must be something *you* want, or why even bother to make a deal with me?" Scarlett was within an arm's length of Raith now. He was still in the same pants and boots he wore to the ball, but his jacket was off now, leaving him in the cream undershirt, the top three buttons undone.

"Clever, girl." He smirked. "I will take Natalie back to the mortal realm if you vow to stay here until the battle is over."

At first, Scarlett's instincts had told her to run away from this place, fast. Then, her curiosity swelled and she decided to learn more of the realm and the fae. But after being drained during the ritual, her intuition was throwing red flags to get the hell out of there again. If she agreed to this, she might never make it home.

"I thought humans couldn't be held here against their will?" That's what Cade had told her. "I'll convince Natalie to ask to go home."

"True, but when someone is taking away all your pain, leaving becomes *difficult*."

The memory of her mother crept in and pressed against her heart. The pain she'd been running from since it happened was what brought her here in the first place. Scarlett wanted to think she was strong enough to leave now, but even if she was, she couldn't leave Natalie here.

"I agree to stay until the battle is over and you take Natalie back and never bring her here again." Scarlett had to be careful. Bargains were tricky. She had to cover all her bases.

"*I* will never bring her back, but I can't guarantee she won't find another way. For all the dangers we fae present, humans aren't very good at staying away once they've felt it here in Faerie."

So, if Scarlett made this deal and then Natalie was desperate to have her emotion fed from again, she could find another fae. Would that be difficult? Or were fae everywhere, eagerly waiting for a new human to prey on?

Cade had said Raith's power laid in memories.

"Then take away her memory of this place," Scarlett said. It was better that way. Then it would be as if she was never here and she would have never seen Scarlett. But taking away someone's memory without her consent seemed low. But it was for Natalie's own protection, Scarlett convinced herself.

"I could, but I'd need something else in return."

"What?"

Raith shrugged. "How about…a kiss?"

"Just one kiss?" Was there some trick behind it? What harm could come from a kiss?

"One measly kiss and it will be as if Natalie never saw any of this." Raith gestured to the ballroom.

"Why? Why all this trouble to make sure I don't leave until after the battle?" Scarlett was just a mortal, and the importance, or lack thereof, of humans in this world was apparent.

"You're making this whole battle far more interesting," Raith said. "So, do we have a deal?"

"Deal."

"We'll seal it with the kiss." Raith stepped toward Scarlett and placed his hands on her hips.

Scarlett looked up. A grin molded on his lips.

"Don't look so miserable, love." Raith leaned in and pulled Scarlett's body into his.

Her chest pressed into his as his hands moved to her face.

Scarlett closed her eyes.

His tongue grazed her bottom lip before his mouth crushed into hers.

Scarlett's instinct took over as she kissed him back. Their mouths moved feverishly as his hands roamed her body, grazing gently over her breasts and moving on to her waist.

This was pure passion, more than anything Scarlett had felt in her entire life. Her hands combed his hair.

And then he pulled back, a smirk on his face. "Well, that was…"

"Get Natalie home safely and make her forget it all," Scarlett's tone was bitter. But it wasn't Raith that she was furious at; it was herself. It was supposed to be a quick kiss. Not whatever that was.

"As you wish." Raith's index finger brushed over his lips as a smirk formed on his mouth. "And Scarlett? Should you ever grow tired of my little brother, I can take your pain away better than he can."

He disappeared before she could refuse him with some colorful words.

Scarlett wiped her mouth as she walked back up the stairs. She could still taste Raith's mouth on hers.

And she didn't hate it.

Chapter Eighteen

C ade's magic buzzed through him as Poppy swung a dagger at his throat. He blocked it with his sword, twisting her dagger away from his face.

Ever since he inhaled Scarlett's pain during the ritual, power surged through Cade. Her emotion had always been delicious, but with the added effect of the ritual, it was the most delectable thing he'd ever tasted. And she was his, not his brother's. That alone made him happy, but everything would be even better when he defeated Raith in the upcoming battle.

Poppy sliced at Cade's stomach. His sword clinked against her dagger. She swiped her other dagger at his neck, stopping before she severed his jugular.

How was she such a good fighter? With magic blazing through him, he thought he'd have an advantage. Apparently not.

"You're getting better, but your sword is still too slow."

Poppy retracted her blade. "You should practice with the bow and arrow."

Cade groaned. He'd always hated the bow. "The sword might be slow, but with a bow and arrow Raith would defeat me in mere seconds."

"Not for the battle," Poppy snapped. "For The Hunt."

Right, The Hunt. Cade would have the pleasure of chasing down a boar. He couldn't contain his excitement.

As Cade shot arrows across the room at a target, missing nearly every time, Poppy gave him some tips. "The boar will be drawn to the creek, so if you find the water, follow it."

"Got it." Another miss, but at least this one was respectably close.

"What's going on with this human girl you've brought here?" It was the first time Poppy mentioned Scarlett.

"She refills my magic."

But it was more than that. Sure, the main benefit to Scarlett was the ecstasy of magic she filled Cade with, but something else about her soothed him. He hadn't felt as relaxed as he did the other day when he took her to the beach behind the castle in years. Maybe ever.

Duty. It was the pressure he'd felt his whole life. He was a prince—with certain expectations heaped upon him at birth. His older brother flew through life on a careless wind, but Cade wanted his people to respect him. Most of all, he didn't want to disappoint his mother.

"And that's all?" Poppy asked.

Cade shrugged. He shot another arrow, this time

through the target's center. "That's the most important part."

A flicker of curiosity shot through Poppy's eyes, but she didn't ask any more questions about Scarlett. Instead, she brought up Raith. "And what's the story behind you and your brother?"

"What story?"

"You seem...distant."

Cade chuckled. "You're quite the observant one."

"He's going to try to get into your head," Poppy said. "During the battle."

Raith would try. He always tried to stir Cade up. But Cade would keep his focus and show his brother just how powerful he had become.

***

THINGS WEREN'T ALWAYS bad with Scarlett's mom. In her lucid moments, her mom was her best friend. Someone she could go to about anything, no matter how embarrassing or taboo it was.

After Scarlett broke things off with Teddy, she was a mess. She spent the entire weekend in her bed, unable to eat or drink more than just a sip of water here and there. It was pathetic, really, because Scarlett was the one who broke up with him. But it wasn't because Teddy wasn't great—he was too wonderful. Scarlett was a mess when it came to guys. She didn't want to brush her curse onto Teddy.

On Monday morning, despite feeling like a zombie as

Scarlett went through the motions of getting ready for school, her mom barged into her room and told her it was a sick day for them both. She told Scarlett to put her pajamas back on and come out to the living room.

Her mom made French toast for breakfast, with strawberries and syrup *and* whipped cream. *"Breakups require lots of sugar,"* she told Scarlett. They made themselves comfortable on the couch, Scarlett wrapped up in her favorite hot pink fleece blanket, and spent the morning watching soap operas and mocking the sheer cheesiness of them.

Afterward, Scarlett's mom asked her what had happened.

Scarlett told her she was too afraid to ruin something good, so she broke it off before anything amazing could happen.

Scarlett's mom pulled her into a hug. "My girl, you aren't damaged goods. Not at all. Any guy would be lucky to have you, no matter how it all turned out. You can't worry about the future like that."

Scarlett squeezed her mom, thankful for a normal mother-daughter moment. Despite the unpredictably of Scarlett's mom, she loved her more than anything.

"Now, it's chick flick time." Her mom switched the TV to Netflix and they browsed the romantic comedy section until they agreed on a movie.

Maybe things were looking up. Her mom had been stable for a while.

Scarlett's hope was shattered a week later when she came home and found her mom on the floor.

Chapter Nineteen

A week after the opening ceremony, Raith sat on the edge of his bed in the castle and pulled his black leather boots on. With everyone coming to witness The Hunt, he had decided to spend the night inside the castle instead of in his tree. This room had three windows, allowing plenty of light to enter. It was too grandiose for his taste. It could fit at least three more monstrous four-poster beds, maybe even four. Don't even get him started on the decorations. Gold, gaudy picture frames held pictures of creepy fae children playing in the courtyard. He preferred the coziness of his house under the tree. The small fireplace could light the entire room. This fireplace, on the other hand, was too far away from the bed to do much good.

With a sigh, he stood and left the room.

Raith didn't understand why so many people cared to come to this event. It wasn't as if they could see The Hunt itself. He and Cade would be in the dark forest, searching for a fucking boar. What better way to have two brothers duke it out than to have them hunt for dinner? Seriously, who'd decided that?

No point in complaining now. Unless he wanted to hand the Right of Heir to Cade, he'd have to compete in the silly ritual. If he managed to win, at least he could knock his brother's ego down a few notches. Raith made his way to the courtyard. The king and queen sat on the outdoor thrones that had been moved there for the occasion. The same fae that had introduced everyone at the ball stood next to Kassandra. Raith walked up to them, bowed to the king and queen, and waited next to the other fae. A few minutes later, Cade showed up, hand-in-hand with Scarlett, who wore a dazed expression on her face. His brother must have just fed on her.

Raith hadn't seen Scarlett since they'd made the bargain—when they sealed it with that kiss. Its intensity surprised Raith. He could sense that he and Scarlett shared a strong chemistry and had made the kiss part of the deal just to mess with her head. But the sparks between them exploded when their lips met. It made him even more curious about the human, something that could become dangerous.

Another flash of her memory hit him when their lips had met. A woman lay dead on the floor, blood splattered at her sides. It was horrific and Raith pushed it away, then got lost in the passion between them. But in that short moment, the pain he experienced felt like being carved alive with the dullest of blades, excruciating and never-ending. It was Scarlett's pain, and now he understood why it had been so easy for Cade to lure her to Faerie.

Raith had done as she wished. He returned Natalie to her home, her memories of Faerie wiped. Even though fixing her pain wasn't part of the deal, Raith felt for the girl. Her silly human vanity was making her miserable. A boyfriend had told her to lose weight, and that tiny seed had sprouted into an entire garden of self-doubt. Raith didn't like messing with memories—it usually brought guilt, as if he were meddling in things he shouldn't. But he saw Natalie's vibrant self when her pain had been dulled from his feeding, so he erased the fat comment, too.

Scarlett's eyes met his.

He winked, and he swore she held back a smile.

"Welcome," the announcer spoke. "We are ready to begin."

The crowd quieted, their gazes shifting to Raith and Cade.

The fae continued. "We are here to witness The Hunt. Both brothers will be fighting to be the one to spear the beast. But to make things more interesting, each will take a serum that blocks his mental shields against the forest."

Well, shit. How did Raith not know that part? From the wide-eyed look on Cade's face, he must have been surprised, too.

The announcer took out two vials of liquid, the same size as what Scarlett took at the ball. But this liquid was emerald. He handed them to Raith and Cade.

"After you take the liquid, you will be evanesced into a cordoned off section of the forest. The only creatures allowed inside are you two and the beast. Neither of you may leave until the beast is speared. You will each be given a spear and a bow with magically refilling arrows as well as a horse."

How hard could it be? Raith lifted his vial into the air. "Cheers, brother."

He gulped down the liquid, which tingled as it went down. It tasted like a pinecone. Raith gagged.

He heard the announcer wish him good luck before he vanished and appeared inside the forest. Raith had been in the dark forest many times, but never this far in. The trees remained still around him, not even a bird on their branches. He heard a rustle behind him. Raith flipped around, arms raised in front of him. A black horse was tied to a tree. Its dark mane shined. Raith recognized him. It was Theo, his favorite horse from the stables. It had been, what, three years since Raith had last ridden? He'd been so busy practicing with weapons and his battle magic he didn't think of tuning up his horseback riding skills.

"Hi, Theo." Raith patted Theo's neck. "Good boy.

Propped against a tree were a spear and a bow and arrow, just as the announcer had promised. Raith slung the bow over his shoulder and fastened the spear in front of Theo's saddle. Raith stuck his foot in the stirrup and grabbed onto the saddle horn then pulled himself up. He grasped the rains and gave Theo a gentle kick, and they were off.

He'd missed this, the feeling of the breeze as they galloped. Now, all he needed to do was find the boar, shoot it, and be done.

As they rode through the trees, something shifted ahead. Was it Cade? Or maybe the beast?

"Woah, boy." Raith slowed Theo down to a trot.

Something grew out of the ground—tree roots. They climbed higher and snaked toward Raith. He tried to back Theo up, but the tree was faster. The roots circled Raith, binding him in place.

His arms struggled against the bonds with no luck. He was stuck. Theo kept still beneath him.

No, this couldn't be happening. It wasn't real. Raith remembered the liquid he drank. His mental shields were down and the forest had strong mind magic. This was an illusion—and a powerful one. Raith again fought to break the hold. No luck. Fuck.

His mental shields had been strong for so long, he'd forgotten the influence the forest could have. He'd been able to defeat it before. He could do it again. A squawking noise caught Raith's attention. A raven sat upon a branch. Another joined. Then another. Their screeching grew louder and louder. Raith felt something drip from his nose. Blood.

He closed his eyes. This wasn't real. It was an illusion meant to distract him. He emptied his mind, inhaling a deep breath. His brain pictured the forest as it was before, calm, with no attacking roots or loud birds.

When he opened his eyes, everything was back to normal.

IT HAD BEEN an hour and no sign of Raith or Cade spearing the beast. The announcer had told the crowd that once it had been killed, the three would appear back in the courtyard.

Scarlett watched fae talk amongst themselves as they waited for something to happen. She had thought the ball was full of fae, but there were at least twice as many here now. The ball had been adults only, but now children ran around their parents, trying to make the most of their freedom.

She wondered if the fae lived their lives like humans did. Did they marry and raise a family? Work a job to pay bills? Or did magic make everything easier? She didn't even know if all the fae had magic.

Since Raith and Cade had disappeared, Scarlett kept quiet a few feet from the thrones. When she'd first arrived, she had been drained from Cade's feeding of her emotion. But as she waited, her brain cleared, which had been happening faster the longer she'd been in Faerie.

Kassandra had a human servant bring her a glass of wine, which had been magically refilled three times now. The king sat in his throne, back straight and glossy-eyed. He hadn't spoken, not even when the servant asked if he'd like wine, too. His expression remained forward as if he looked for something off in the distance.

Scarlett felt odd just standing there, but she wasn't sure where else to go. Occasionally, she'd catch the gaze of someone in the crowd. Some eyed her curiously, probably wondering who in the hell she was to be accompanying a fae prince everywhere. Some glared. Some seemed to pretend she didn't even exist.

Kassandra motioned for her servant. "Bring me a plate of fruit. I'm famished."

The servant, around Scarlett's age, nodded and rushed off, brown eyes full of panic. Her black hair was pulled into a bun that accentuated her long neck. She came back with a platter of grapes and apples.

"Where are the strawberries?" Kassandra asked as the servant tried to hand her the plate.

"I…They…" She replied.

"I won't accept it until there are strawberries." Kassandra shooed the servant girl with a brush of her hand.

She hurried away and came back with strawberries on the plate. Kassandra took it this time, with no thank you. The girl returned to the side of the crowd.

"What are you staring at, human?" Kassandra turned her head toward Scarlett.

Scarlett hadn't realized she'd been staring, but her gaze had been focused on the queen as the servant had given her the fruit. "Nothing. Sorry."

"Come here."

Scarlett stepped slowly toward her. She didn't have much of a choice. Disobeying the queen's orders wouldn't win her any favor, no matter whom she supposedly belonged to. As she walked, she straightened out her dress. When she reached Kassandra, she curtsied to her and then to the king, who didn't even blink. What was wrong with him?

"For whatever reason, you've been blessed with misery that helps my son."

Scarlett just stared at her. Did she expect her to respond to that with *you're welcome that I'm miserable?*

Kassandra flicked her index finger. "Come closer."

Scarlett leaned in, a mere foot from Kassandra's face. The queen's smooth skin was flawless, with not a single blemish. How old was she? Scarlett was sure there were many aging women in the human world that would kill for such perfection.

Kassandra's eyes started at Scarlett's hair and worked their way down to her chest, which, at the angle she was bent, was exposed to the cool air. "You're attractive—for a human. Most are hideous. And so desperate. The things they'll let you do to escape their emotions. Death, heartbreak, disease. Humans run."

"You can heal disease?"

"Of course not. But we can take away the fear of dying. Fear is one of the best flavors of emotion if you ask me."

So, even the fae couldn't have saved her mother.

Scarlett stood there awkwardly, not sure what to do or say.

Kassandra sighed. "You are lucky my son has given you his attention. To be a prince's human is something many mortals would kill for. Now leave."

She didn't have to tell Scarlett twice. Kassandra gave her the creeps. Scarlett went back to standing alone as she waited for The Hunt to end. Another hour passed. Her feet ached. How long did it take to shoot a boar?

A servant brought Kassandra another plate of fruit, but she stumbled and dropped the plate. As Scarlett watched her rush to pick up everything she had spilled, someone appeared next to Scarlett, grabbed her hand, and Scarlett felt herself pulled away.

Her body felt like a feather moving through the wind, unable to control her direction. Then her feet found the ground. Nausea grew in her stomach. What had happened?

"Just breathe, the nausea goes away," Kaelem said next to her as he released her hand. Like at the ball, he wore a sleek suit. This one was white with a lavender shirt underneath and a white tie. If his hair wasn't navy, Scarlett may have thought he was a Wall Street broker or some other human professional. Or more like a model pretending to be one.

Scarlett looked around. They weren't near the crowd anymore. Somehow, they'd travelled to the courtyard. "What was that?"

"Evanescing."

"Sorry, what?"

"Moving from one place to another incredibly fast."

Scarlett took a step. The ground felt hard beneath her feet, like after getting off a treadmill. After a few more, she walked normally. "Where are we?"

"The other side of the castle."

"Why?"

"Your feet were hurting." Kaelem motioned to a small fountain. "Have a seat."

"And what do you care? Surely a fae king has better things to do than rescue some human."

Kaelem shrugged as he sat on the fountain ledge. "Are you going to join?"

Scarlett glared at him. Why she was mad, she wasn't sure. Ever since she made that bargain with Raith, she'd been in a foul mood anytime she remembered. She wasn't sure why she cared so much. It's not like she'd been begging Cade to let her leave, but she felt better knowing she *could* ask him to take her away. Then again, deep down, she knew he wouldn't take her home without a fight. He'd make her feel all the pain at once until she begged him to take it away, thoughts of leaving disappeared.

"God, these brothers really have you bothered, don't they?" Kaelem ran his fingers through the fountain water. "And you've kissed them both. How scandalous!"

"Get out of my head." Scarlett gritted her teeth as she spoke, trying not to think any more incriminating thoughts. If Cade found out about her bargain with Raith, or worse, the kiss... Scarlett didn't want to even contemplate what might happen.

"Come, sit, and I'll get out," Kaelem said. "For now, at least."

Scarlett dragged her feet but took a seat next to him. "Do you have some secret plan to drown me in the fountain?"

Kaelem laughed. "You're so paranoid. No, darling, I have no intention of drowning you. I'd have both summer princes after me then."

Scarlett rolled her eyes. "A human death would be nothing more than a hiccup to them."

"Maybe, but they seem awfully attached to you."

Scarlett crossed her right leg over her left. She'd rather sprawl out on the grass but that didn't seem very ladylike and wasn't practical in her dress. "Is that why you're so interested in me? You want to piss them off?"

"My, my. Why would I ever want to do that?" The gleam in his eyes told Scarlett he'd have no problem making waves with Raith or Cade. She looked deeper into his eyes then her gaze travelled to his lips. God they looked delicious, like caramel on an apple just waiting to be licked.

Stop, Scarlett.

Head out of the gutter.

What was it about him?

He didn't react to her dirty thoughts so he must actually be out of her head now. Shocker. Scarlett didn't think he'd actually keep his word. "Then why bring me here?"

"Summer fae bore me, and The Hunt was taking forever, so I figured I'd get us out of there. You looked to be having a more miserable time than I was."

"You must have been bored if you're wanting to spend time with a mortal."

Kaelem just shrugged. "What brings you to the Summer Court? You don't seem the typical desperate human that they usually lure in."

Was that a compliment?

The image of her mom being carted away by the

paramedics surfaced. Her chest clenched. Then the tightness slowly disappeared.

"You're taking my pain, aren't you?" Scarlett asked.

He didn't answer. "So, something bad happened and you're running away?"

"I'm not running…" But that's exactly what she was doing. She and Ashleigh fought after yet another failed attempt at visiting her mom's grave, and suddenly a miracle showed up to take her away—to an entirely new realm, nonetheless. "So what if I am?"

Kaelem stood. "No judgment here, darling. Only mere curiosity. I have a habit of learning the nuances of the other courts. Keeps me up-to-date should information ever be needed."

Scarlett got lost in his eyes again. Then her eyes wandered down past his face, to his chest, then lower…

What was wrong with her? Being around him might be dangerous. Scarlett pushed herself up from the fountain ledge.

"Finding yourself…enticed?" Kaelem said.

"I thought you were staying out of my head." Scarlett lifted her gaze back to his face.

His eyebrow arched, curious. Something gleamed in his gaze, an awareness of some sort.

"Oh, I am. But you're practically drooling." The smirk on his face let Scarlett know he knew something he wasn't telling her.

"Is there a reason I'm having… improper thoughts?" Scarlett clenched her teeth, embarrassed at the confession.

"Since you asked nicely, I'm a ganacanagh." Kaelem's eyes danced. "A fae with especially *potent* sex appeal."

Lovely. At least it explained Scarlett's foul thoughts. Not that Kaelem wasn't attractive enough to warrant lust without any extra gift—he was a fae after all. *And* a king. Seriously, what was with all these fae royals giving their attention to Scarlett? She was a mortal. Only, she knew that might not be true.

Not only had she felt emotion radiating off of others —including Cade—but she'd always wondered if something was *different* about her. Not to mention the dagger orb had lit up in her hands. For her to have intrigued three fae royals, she must have something to offer that other mortals didn't.

Then again, she might just be a silly prize they all were desperate to win.

"Too bad you've already promised to stay here in the Summer Court," Kaelem said. "I could have helped you out of here."

Sure, now that Scarlett couldn't leave he offered his help. Typical. "I thought you were afraid of starting a battle with the Summer princes."

Kaelem shrugged. "A little drama never killed anybody."

He leaned his body into hers, his breath hot in her face. His lips puckered ever-so-slightly. A mouth so perfect needed to be kissed…

Scarlett shook her head side-to-side, banishing the lustful thoughts.

Kaelem grinned, then whispered, "I can see what the

Summer princes see in you. The Unseelie Court could offer you so much more." His tone sang of temptation and sinful promise. "Maybe someday you'll come visit me and I can show your what it's really like to have a good time."

Scarlett took three steps back and snapped her gaze away from the Unseelie King. He was dangerous, in more ways than one.

The Hunt couldn't be over soon enough.

Chapter Twenty

❧❧❧

Cade tied the brown mare to a tree. He'd tried to ride her while looking for the beast, but the stubborn creature wouldn't listen to the command of the reigns. He never liked horseback riding. As children, Raith would ride like the wind while Cade feared even a trot. And right now, Cade didn't have time for the struggle. He'd be faster on foot.

He meandered through the trees, careful to keep his steps quiet lest he scare the boar away. It had to have been a couple of hours of searching by now and he hadn't seen it. Not even once. Thankfully, he hadn't run into Raith yet, either, and since Cade was still in the forest, Raith must not have shot the beast.

Something moved on a tree as he passed it. It circled down the trunk, and, when it hit the ground, Cade realized it was a snake. While on the tree, its skin was brown, but once it hit the forest floor, it turned a bright green. Cade backed up slowly at first, but the snake picked up its pace. As Cade turned to run away, a tree root popped up from underground and Cade stumbled over it.

The snake grew larger until it was at least twenty feet long. What was happening? Cade couldn't get up in time, and the snake twirled itself around him, squeezing him tight. The announcer said there weren't any other creatures in this part of the forest, so how was a snake holding Cade captive?

He recalled the liquid he drank. His mental shields were down. Of course. This wasn't real.

Then he saw the boar, only a few feet away. Was *it* real, or was the forest toying with him? The beast ran away into the woods. The snake squeezed tighter. The forest was only messing with his head. He just needed to think of something else. Something good. Scarlett's face popped into his head—the way her dark hair brought out the blue in her eyes. How when she smiled, her eyes squinted. Cade released the tension inside him with an exhale of breath.

The snake and tree root vanished.

Cade pushed himself up and jogged the direction the boar had gone. He saw its footprints in the dirt. It had been real. The footprints disappeared and Cade wasn't sure which way to go, so he kept moving straight.

Ahead, he saw a black stallion, Raith sitting on top, his bow aimed at the boar. Of course his brother still rode on his horse, giving him the advantage of height. Cade needed to think quickly or he was about to lose.

"Run," Cade yelled, hoping to scare the beast.

It started to dash away. Cade created a ball of summer

energy in his hand and threw it at his brother. But his aim was high and Raith ducked out of the way.

Cade tried to run toward the boar, but his right foot stepped on a branch and slipped, sending him face forward to the ground. Of all the times for him to fall.

When he looked up, Raith adjusted his aim again. As Cade screamed at the creature, Raith let the arrow go. It sailed through the air and found the boar's heart. Cade glared at his brother, who returned the stare with a wink.

Within a breath, Cade was evanesced back into the courtyard. He appeared next to Raith, the beast dead on the ground in front of them.

"The winner of The Hunt is Prince Raith," the announcer said.

The crowd applauded.

Cade looked to his mother who wore a scowl. This was only one part of the Battle of Heirs, and it didn't even count for much. She shouldn't be so upset. The winner of the actual battle would be king, not the one who did nothing but shoot a boar. Maybe this would raise Raith's confidence and Cade could take advantage during the battle.

He searched for Scarlett but didn't see her. Raith may have won The Hunt, but Scarlett was still Cade's. Where could she have gone?

Scarlett stepped out from behind the thrones and walked to him.

He pulled her close to him. The Hunt was stupid. Cade didn't know why he even cared that he lost. He would be the stronger brother in the end.

"Come," he said to her. "Let's go to your room."

CADE'S MOUTH pressed against Scarlett's as he guided her to the bed. He motioned the door shut with his magic.

In between kisses, she leaned her face back.

"Are you okay?" she asked, her forehead crinkled.

"I just want to take my mind off of the Right of Heir." Cade reached around Scarlett and unbuttoned her dress.

"You're upset, let's talk." She put her hands on his chest.

Fine, if she didn't want to be physical, Cade would find another way to strengthen himself. "I don't feel like *talking*, but just lie with me?"

Scarlett nodded. She took her dress off and tossed it over a chair in the corner, then crawled under the covers of her bed. After Cade joined her, she curled up next to him.

As her head rested on his chest, he ran his fingers up and down her arm. She closed her eyes as she snuggled closer to his body. He searched for her pain, but he couldn't find much. She was so much less *troubled* than usual. What had she done while he was busy with The Hunt?

Raith was in the forest with him, or Cade would have worried his brother had gotten under her skin. Since bringing Scarlett to Faerie, he'd noticed her improvement. She wasn't overflowing with grief as she had been when he first saw her overlooking the cemetery. If she continued to let go of her pain, she wouldn't be as good of a magic source for Cade.

He couldn't have that.

She peered up, gaze heavy. She parted her lips as if to say something, then snapped them shut and sighed.

Cade moved the finger tracing her arm to her cheek, gently grazing her soft skin. She exhaled and shut her eyes again.

Once she dozed off, Cade closed his eyes and entered her dreamland.

SCARLETT WAS IN A MORTAL BEDROOM, sitting on the bed as another girl glanced at herself in the mirror. Bright colors filled the room—hot pink pillows, a shaggy teal rug, a lavender accent wall behind the white headboard.

"You sure it looks okay?" the girl said. When she turned, Cade recognized her—the girl Raith had brought to the ball, Natalie.

Cade focused. Normally when he entered dreams, he physically became part of them. It allowed him to seduce humans, sleep with them, and then leave. No harm, no foul. But Cade had a different idea. He wanted to feel the high of being fully replenished, and though sex gave him power, Scarlett's pain was a strong source, too. He searched her mind for fear.

The room shifted, and now Scarlett was back in the room she had went to during the ritual. Her mother was dead on the floor. Scarlett searched for a pulse that couldn't be found. The pain sweltered inside Scarlett's head. Regret, confusion, anger all swirled together to create a delicious magical meal.

Cade inhaled it, feeling it refuel him.

He'd take a gulp of pain then let it build inside her again before having more. Over and over he did this as her mother faded away in her mind.

The scene changed again. Scarlett in another bedroom, but this time she was with her sister who shouted at her.

"It's all your fault, Scarlett," Ashleigh said. "If you'd have been a better daughter Mom wouldn't have killed herself."

"That's not true." Tears streamed down Scarlett's face.

Cade breathed in the pain.

"You stressed her out all the time. Seriously, what kind of person are you?" her sister yelled.

She kept throwing insults at Scarlett who could do nothing to stop her. Instead, tears poured from her eyes.

Cade chugged and chugged the emotion, power bursting inside him.

Then Scarlett's dream went black.

CADE JUMPED out of her mind and looked at her lying next to him in the bed. He'd taken things too far, causing her to black out. He should feel bad, but the magic inside him sent ecstasy through his veins. He was too high to feel. Too powerful.

His brother might have one the silly Hunt, but he'd seen nothing of what Cade was capable of. He held his hands out in front of himself, face up. A green orb glowed in his palms.

With summer magic this strong, there was no way he'd lose the battle.

Chapter Twenty-One

S carlett awoke alone in Cade's bed, her eyelids heavy. She remembered falling asleep in his arms, and then she remembered her dreams. She felt sick to her stomach. Why did she dream such horrible things? She'd come to this place to get away from those feelings, but lately they'd been resurfacing more and more, more often and stronger than ever. Now more than ever she wanted to get home, but after making the bargain with Raith, she was stuck here. Once the battle was over, she'd be ready. Until then, she'd play the part she needed to play.

"Good morning," Cade said as he walked through the door.

"Make it stop." Scarlett pleaded with her eyes. The memories made her dizzy. She'd felt in control yesterday, like maybe she was starting to handle the pain. But a night of dreams had torn the hope from her.

Cade sat on the bed next to her and placed her hand in his. The emotion inside Scarlett emptied until her mind was clear again, like a weight had been lifted from her thoughts.

She thought of her mother and her sister but felt nothing but numbness. It was better this way.

"I have battle practice this morning," Cade said, hand still twined with Scarlett's. "Will you be all right?"

Sometimes he acted like she was nothing more than a pet. Other times, like now, he treated her like she was someone he cared about. It confused her, but she wouldn't let it bother her. Her worries were too far away at the moment for *anything* to bother her right then.

"I'll be fine." She withdrew her hand and pushed herself out of the bed. "I may go outside and explore the castle grounds, if that's all right."

"Of course. Just don't wander too far. It's dangerous outside the castle walls."

Scarlett looked to the scar on her leg. She knew all too well the trouble she would find if she tried to leave. Somehow, she had escaped the creature, but she still wasn't sure how. And there'd be no point in running now. She *couldn't* leave, not with the bargain she'd made with Raith, which she wasn't about to share with Cade. She didn't know exactly what happened when someone broke a fae bargain, and she had no desire to find out by breaking one.

After Cade left, Scarlett drew herself a bath. As she soaked in the hot water, she thought of her unusual encounter as Cade and Raith competed in The Hunt. For some reason unbeknownst to her, the Unseelie King— apparently a seductive ganacanagh— spent over an hour talking with her. Kaelem asked her questions about her life before entering Faerie—about her family, friends, hobbies. He claimed humans fascinated him. With the Unseelie Court in the mortal realm, he liked to get to know them better, or so he said. Scarlett didn't believe him. He was probably laughing at the mundaneness of the human life.

He offered to answer some of her questions, though.

When she asked him if humans were safe in the Unseelie Court, he bluntly said, "No, humans are never safe around the fae."

Cade had already told her as much, but knowing that two fae courts resided in the mortal realm caused Scarlett to shudder. It was one thing to bring humans here to Faerie, but another for the dangerous creatures to live alongside humans. The Summer Court fae were powerful, but something inside Scarlett screamed that Kaelem was far more of a threat to her than anyone here in Faerie. Cade had said that the Seelie and Unseelie had limited the power of the seasonal courts of Faerie, leaving their fae gifts unrestrained.

Before she could ask anything else, Raith had shot the beast, and Kaelem evanesced Scarlett behind the thrones. Then he vanished. She wasn't even sure why he came to The Hunt. He didn't seem too concerned about who won. Did he care who would be king?

What fascinated Scarlett most was how the courts interacted with each other. Did they feud like European countries did in the sixteenth century? Or did they coexist somewhat peacefully? Scarlett guessed it was more the former, at least if Cade's reaction to Kaelem was any indication. She kept her conversation with Kaelem to herself.

After Scarlett had enough soaking, she got out and dressed. She braided her hair into a French braid, then headed outside. Her head already started to clear, the fog she'd felt after Cade had taken her emotion drifting away. The other day, Cade had shown her the back entrance, which was unguarded. It was magically enchanted as only a castle exit, though, and Scarlett would have to walk around the castle to get back inside. She didn't mind. The weather in Faerie was perfect, at least here in the Summer Court. Like a perfect June day, the sun warmed her skin as a slight breeze blew past.

She exited the castle to the garden, another benefit to the castle's back door. There were rose bushes like the ones on the courtyard, and then there were tulips, chrysanthemums, hydrangea, and peonies. As a child, Scarlett's mother taught her about different types of flowers. Most kids loved picture books, but Scarlett's favorite was a gardening book of her mom's, filled with pictures and descriptions of flowers.

Roses were her mom's favorite flower. She'd spent every morning grooming the rose bushes she had planted along the backside of the house—even when she was off her meds. It was the one consistent thing her mom did. After her mom died, Scarlett tried to keep them healthy, but she didn't inherit her mom's green thumb. Between going to school and doing her homework so she could pass her senior year, Scarlett had little time, and, frankly, gardening just wasn't her thing. Ashleigh would have kept them as perfect as their mom had no matter how busy she was, but she was away at school finishing up her first semester of college.

As Scarlett walked through the garden, she found yellow snapdragons, her favorite—partly because she loved their shape, but mostly because they had the word dragon in them which, as a child, convinced her they were from a magical land. She supposed that, now that she was here, it was true.

The numbness from Cade's feeding had worn off already. She hadn't told him her recovery time improved every day. It was one of the many signs that she wasn't like other humans. Surprisingly, the pain and fear the nightmare had resurfaced was manageable now. This morning she thought it would consume her, but now, she breathed it in and exhaled it into the wind to drift wherever the breeze would take it.

Even though Scarlett knew the danger she was in amongst the supernatural creatures, a part of her felt this place was *right*. It was an unexplainable feeling but one she couldn't ignore. It was beautiful and vibrant in a way she'd never experienced. And it was dangerous which, truthfully, excited her.

For now, she had no choice but to stay. But what about after the battle? Would she ask to remain, and, if so, what would she be to whomever became king?

Or could she finally return home and face her life again?

RAITH SPUN and struck his daggers down onto Jaser's sword.

"Better," Jaser said. "But still predictable."

"We've been training for weeks now." Raith dropped his daggers to his side. "Of course you know my moves."

"And your brother and you used to train together. Won't he know them, too?"

Raith groaned. Would Cade remember how Raith fought? Probably. But he didn't know about Raith's nature magic. Neither did Jaser. During the first training sessions, Raith was convinced Jaser would get on his last nerve. But the more he got to know Jaser, the more Raith realized he wasn't so bad. A brilliant warrior, too.

Maybe even a friend.

Raith had already learned a lot. He wanted to trust Jaser with his nature magic secret, but he couldn't risk it. Maybe Jaser was devoted to helping Raith win the battle now, but allegiances could always change. Cade wouldn't try to bribe Jaser. He would follow the rules and win or lose fairly. Kassandra, on the other hand, would fight dirty, doing whatever she could to assure her little boy's victory.

"How's your summer magic coming along?" Jaser asked.

Raith cupped his hands and thought of his power. A small blue orb appeared and then vanished. "Shitty."

"You'll get it." Jaser hung his sword on the wall. "Eventually."

"Before or after my brother blasts me into oblivion?"

Raith was confident with his nature power, sure, but if he could master his summer power, too, then he'd really be able to show his brother up.

"Past kings have won the battle without their summer magic," Jaser said.

"Yeah, like one out of ten of them."

"Better than none."

A knock on the door interrupted their conversation. Jaser opened it to a male human servant with an envelope in his hand. He grabbed the note and the servant hurried away.

"I don't know why they're so scared of me." Jaser flipped the envelope over. "Looks like it's for you."

Raith flung it through the air to his hands and opened it. Inside was a note from the infirmary saying that the king was drifting away.

Raith crumpled the note in his hand.

"Everything all right?" Jaser's eyebrows furrowed.

"The king is getting worse."

"How is that possible? Fae aren't as frail as humans. We don't get sick."

"No idea."

It wasn't a surprise, really. The king had been going downhill for a while. But never had a king died from this kind of sickness. Raith wasn't close to him, at least not anymore. At one time, he had spent countless hours following the king around. He taught Raith horseback riding. But as Raith got older, Kassandra had gotten in the way. She'd convinced the king that the boys needed to focus on their education. They could worry about royal duties later, when they were older.

"You want to call it a day?" Jaser asked.

Raith lifted his daggers. "The king may not have much longer. All the more reason to train."

Jaser brought a steel staff through the air and to his hands. "Very well."

The two sparred for another hour. At first, Jaser got the best of Raith, tripping him to the ground. Then Raith took Jaser's advice to be less predictable with his movements. Instead of thinking his moves through, he let his body take over, moving with a cat-like grace. Finally, Raith pinned Jaser to the ground with his daggers crossed above Jaser's neck.

"Bravo, prince. Bravo," Jaser said.

Raith helped Jaser up and again, they fought. *Repetition was key*, Jaser repeated over and over.

"To be a strong warrior, everything must become second nature." Jaser lunged from Raith and somersaulted across the room. "Your weapon becomes an extension of your body, your mind free from confliction."

Jaser charged at Raith, sword high above his head. Raith blocked a blow with his daggers. As he pushed Jaser's sword away, Jaser kicked Raith in the stomach, taking the breath from his lungs.

"And always expect the unexpected." Jaser laughed as Raith gave him a vulgar gesture.

After battle practice, Raith headed to the back of the castle to clear his mind. In truth, he wasn't even sure he wanted to be king. Running a court sounded about as fun as being a living dartboard. But he didn't like to lose, least of all to his little brother. Cade and his constant need to be perfect got on Raith's last nerve. Raith believed his little brother had what it took to be a good king, but his momma's boy tendencies could get in the way. Raith didn't trust Kassandra. He never had and likely never would. Perhaps it was just jealousy. Kassandra came into his life so quickly after his own mother died. But he was just a boy who wanted motherly love. Had Kassandra taken him in as her own, maybe Raith would think of her as a mom.

When did he get so sentimental? Fuck. He would win the battle and become king, and then he could do with Kassandra what he pleased. End of story. If only he could figure out the Summer magic.

Raith flung the back castle door open and stepped outside, letting the sunshine pour down on him. It was a nice change after spending three hours in a room of stone. As he walked through the garden, he saw someone through the rosebushes. He closed his eyes and could sense the faint human emotion. It must be Scarlett, drained from Cade's morning feeding. Raith picked a blue snap-dragon from a bush and rounded the corner.

Scarlett didn't notice him at first. She was too busy staring at the rose bush in front of her.

"Hello, love." Raith twirled the flower in his hands.

Scarlett peered up at him, her blue eyes bright. "Stalking me now?"

Raith smirked. "You are rather stalkable."

Scarlett grinned. "That doesn't sound creepy at all."

Raith felt for her emotions. She seemed at ease with him. When she glanced back at the rose bush, he sensed a small burst of pain.

"For you." Raith handed her the snapdragon he picked.

Scarlett took it, her sadness fading ever-so-slightly. "Thank you."

"What brings you out here?" Raith asked. "Planning your escape?"

"I made a bargain to stay." Her expression shifted, sadness settling in her eyes. "Have you upheld your end?"

"Of course, love. Your friend is home safe and won't remember a thing."

"Good." Grief trickled from Scarlett again.

"I must say, that kiss was something else." Raith puckered his lips. "For a human, that is."

A new feeling flowed from Scarlett now: lust. She must have liked it, too. "I aim to please." Her cheeks blushed. "I mean, I'm glad it wasn't bad."

"Anything but."

"I wouldn't have wanted you to back out of our deal. It was nothing more than a business arrangement." The lust buzzing from her told him otherwise.

"We could make a new bargain—one to get you out of here *before* the battle."

For a moment, Scarlett's eyes widened, then they returned to their normal size. "What kind of a bargain?"

"We could start the kiss where we left off, and let it take us where it will." Raith was confident if they kissed again, neither would be able to stop. He was also certain she'd turn him down, but the game was fun nonetheless.

"I'll take my chances here until the battle."

"Very well."

As much as he would have enjoyed taking her right there in that garden, Raith had other plans for Scarlett.

Chapter Twenty-Two

Scarlett kept a smile from appearing on her face. The thought of their kiss made her lips tingle. And his offer was tempting—too tempting. But she'd waited this long to have sex, so there was no way she would lose her virginity in a bargain, no matter how good the sex may be.

"I should be getting back inside now." Scarlett didn't want to have a chance to change her mind.

"If you reconsider." Raith winked.

"I won't."

Scarlett followed the cobblestone path around the castle to its entrance. The guards opened the door for her with their magic without a word. When she got back to her room, a note was waiting for her on her bed. It was an invitation to tea with Kassandra. Great. Her presence was required at noon, in proper attire, whatever that meant. Scarlett picked up the pocket watch from Raith from her bedside table and opened it. It was already eleven thirty. She'd better hurry.

The dress she wore to the gardens was one of the simpler dresses in her closet, and she doubted—despite being nicer than anything she'd ever owned herself—it qualified as nice enough for tea with the Summer Queen. Scarlett slipped into a navy velvet dress instead. She brushed on a little makeup, heavier than she usually wore, and with no time left to do anything different with her hair, made her way to the parlor.

Her stomach clenched. Why would Kassandra want to have tea with her? The queen's distaste for humans was as clear as a cloudless sky. But Scarlett couldn't exactly refuse the invitation. She wasn't some new girlfriend anxious to meet her boyfriend's mother. The situation she found herself in was so much stranger than that and the butterflies in her stomach fluttered harder than any had before.

Kassandra lounged on a cream-colored chaise, her burgundy dress draped carefully, elegant, lovely, and lethal-looking all at once. Across from her was a matching chaise, both next to a marble fireplace.

Something else caught Scarlett's attention: an exquisite grand piano, the fanciest one she'd ever seen, with roses carved into its feet and a glistening sheen emanating from its gloss. Oh how her fingers wanted to glide across its ivory keys. She'd lost herself in playing so many times, and even though pain had kept her away, she still craved the peace it brought. A true peace, not the artificial tranquility she felt after Cade had dulled her pain.

Scarlett approached the queen and curtsied. "Thank you for the invitation."

She wasn't completely sure of fae etiquette yet, but she'd bet that being overly polite was the best option.

Kassandra nodded. "Sit."

Scarlett obliged.

Kassandra clapped her hands. "Music."

From behind the pearl grand piano in the corner of the room, a fae man began to play a song with an upbeat tempo. Scarlett resisted the urge to wiggle her fingers to the beat.

Kassandra hummed along. "Ah, isn't it lovely?"

"Very." Scarlett folded her hands in her lap, catching her thumb twitching to the music every so often.

A girl servant came into the room, a silver platter with a teapot and cups in her hand—the same girl who brought Kassandra fruit during the hunt. She carefully set the platter on the table between the chaises and poured the tea. Slowly, she handed Kassandra hers first and then Scarlett's. Her anxiousness spread through the air like strong perfume, invisible to the eye but unavoidably obvious just the same.

"Thank you," Scarlett said.

"Off you go," Kassandra said. "Bring us fruit."

"Yes, my queen." The servant hurried away.

Kassandra sipped her tea. "So, what did your human existence consist of?"

"Um… school, family, friends?" She wasn't sure what Kassandra meant, so Scarlett kept her answer general.

"And what do they teach you in human school?"

"English, math, science, history. Lots of stuff."

"Lots of *stuff*. How eloquent." Kassandra set her teacup on the table and reclined in the chaise.

"Humans have learned a lot. We've been to the moon, medical science has progressed incredibly, and technology is growing all the time." Scarlett didn't like to be thought of as some idiot just because she was human. She made a mental note to select words from her vocabulary more wisely from now on.

"And yet they get drunk and drive into trees."

"Have you been to the mortal realm?" Asking the queen a question was bold, but Scarlett couldn't resist. She couldn't picture Kassandra walking down a city street as cars passed her by.

"Once, and that was *more* than enough for an eternity."

The servant returned with a platter of fruit. She placed it on the table. "Can I refill your tea, my queen?"

"Yes."

The girl picked up the teapot and began pouring. Her arm jerked to the right and the tea fell, splashing all over the stone floor.

"I'm so sorry." The girl's voice shook.

Fear emanated from the servant. It was as if electricity shot through Scarlett's nerves, sending adrenaline coursing through her veins. It was power and energy and alertness.

A spoon rose from the table and shot into the girl's arm. She squealed. Blood dripped from the wound like tears, pooling into a red puddle on the table.

"Your clumsiness will not be tolerated."

Tears overflowed in the servant's eyes. Scarlett inhaled her panic, sending a jolt to her core. What was happening?

"Now, *leave*." Kassandra's expression was flat. She didn't have to ask twice. The girl turned around and rushed out of the room. "Humans are so inept."

Scarlett ground her teeth but kept her mouth shut. The girl didn't spill that tea on her own. Scarlett saw her arm flicked away.

"Finish your tea. It's rude not to drink it all." Kassandra watched Scarlett as she gulped the rest. "Some of you are quite stubborn. Please know you're only welcome here because my son has taken a fondness to you and you're able to help him grow stronger for the battle. This is not a fairytale where the prince falls for the human girl and they live happily ever after. If you do anything to get in the way of Cade winning the Right of Heir, I'll have you and anyone you've ever cared about hunted."

Scarlett believed every word.

With her cup now empty, she put it on the table. "Thank you for the lovely tea, but I should be going now."

Scarlett rose from the chaise and left without another word. She knew Kassandra meant her threat. What happened if Cade became king? Would he let her go home? What about Raith?

A crying noise pulled Scarlett out of her thoughts. Scarlett could feel the servant's fear, drifting like a trail of smoke. She followed it to under the stairs where the girl sat in the darkness. Her hand clung to her arm, the spoon still stuck in her flesh.

"Come with me," Scarlett said. Who knew what would happen if Kassandra found her under here. Scarlett walked as fast as she could, her elbow linked with the servant as she pulled her to her room. When they were inside, she shut the door. "The more you show her your fear, the more she'll go after you."

A classic habit of all bullies. Kassandra was more than some jerk on the playground, she was a queen with the magic and status to do almost anything she wanted to anyone she wanted.

The girl glared. "You've been here how long and you already know everything?"

"Sorry, I'm just trying to help." The girl was right, though. Scarlett didn't know anything about her.

The girl sniffled. "The servants all hate you. Suddenly a human comes in that the fae treat with actual decency while we're all basically slaves." Her tone was free from coldness and was very matter-of-fact.

"I thought they couldn't have humans as slaves anymore." Cade had said humans had to come willingly, which wasn't exactly slavery. Scarlett took the girl's arm into her hand and looked over the spoon. As the servant's arm shifted, Scarlett could feel the pain bursting from her. Like before, she inhaled it.

"Technically we're indentured servants. We all made a deal with one of them and here we are until the bargain is fulfilled. No take-backs if we changed our minds."

Scarlett thought of her deal with Raith. He could have asked her to stay a lot longer and she'd have agreed— anything to save Natalie. Why hadn't he?

"What are you?" The girl stared at Scarlett.

"I'm sorry?" Scarlett didn't know what she meant.

"I can feel you subduing my pain. Like they can."

Was that what Scarlett was doing? She could feel something building inside herself. Was it magic of some sort?

"I don't know." Scarlett's eyes met hers. Scarlett sucked in her pain as much as she could and yanked the spoon from the girl's arm.

The girl winced but didn't scream. Blood seeped from the wound. Scarlett wasn't sure how she knew to do what she was about to do, but something in her told her to place her hand over the cut, so she did. She envisioned the girl's arm back to normal, and when she removed her hand, except for the blood, it was as if the spoon had never touched her.

Shock covered the girl's face. She ran a finger where the wound had been. "How did you do that?"

"Something just told me I could." God, she sounded outright mad, but then again, it worked. The energy that had been buzzing inside Scarlett after she absorbed the girl's pain had dulled. "I'm Scarlett, by the way."

"I know," the girl snapped. Then she relaxed. "I'm Abigail."

"Do other humans ever have *gifts*?" Scarlett asked. Surely, she couldn't be the only one.

Abigail shook her head. "No, humans don't have power."

Then what was Scarlett? Did she even want to know?

"Thank you." Abigail admired her arm. "I better get back to work."

"Put a fake bandage on it," Scarlett said. "So Kassandra doesn't stick it back in."

"Good idea." Abigail hesitated at the door. After she was out the door, she turned back. "Don't let them know what you can do."

Chapter Twenty-Three

S carlett kept her lips sealed, and since no one questioned her about her sudden ability, Abigail must have kept it quiet, too. Her days blurred together. Every night she dreamed of her mother, and every morning Cade sucked her pain away. But the numbness wore away quicker each day. She spent most of her days walking around the castle grounds or reading a book in the library.

She still hadn't gotten used to the fact that, for now, she lived in a castle. The luxurious décor and sheer size of her room still awed her, but when she went outside and looked at the stone exterior, she was even more amazed. She'd always wanted to visit Europe and tour a medieval castle to experience a small taste of what it was like for royals living at the time. But this was so much more. This castle wasn't a museum—with rules to follow and a tour guide keeping her on an allowed path. And this castle had *magic*.

Cade had been spending all his time practicing, and since Scarlett hadn't seen Raith around, she guessed he'd been preparing, too. Today, exactly one week before the battle, was The Blessing. Cade wouldn't bring a date this time, but he told her she was welcome to join the crowd and watch.

At first Scarlett planned to stay in her room, cuddled in bed with a book. Then her curiosity won out. How many humans could say they witnessed a fae blessing? Then again, she wasn't so sure she *was* a human. All the more reason she should learn as much as she could.

Scarlett went to the bottom floor of the castle and snuck into the crowd of Summer fae, all eager for The Blessing to begin. She wore an obsidian chiffon dress with a matching headscarf, an attempt to hide her identity. She was tired of all the stares—from both fae and humans alike—as if she were some social pariah. To her surprise, people seemed to notice her less than they had at The Hunt.

The announcer stood on the balcony. Cade and Raith each stood to one of his sides. Kassandra sat in a throne to their side. Sometimes, Scarlett could see the resemblance between them. Other times, like now, they looked nothing like one another. Cade's posture was perfect, his expression still. His black jacket was embellished with gold embroidery. Raith leaned his head to one side as he yawned. He outfit looked regal, but in a different way. His hunter green jacket was plainer than his brothers, velvet in material but without any frills.

"Welcome, Summer Court," the announcer said.

"The Summer Court High Priest has arrived to give The Blessing."

A fae dressed in a white robe stepped to the front of the balcony. A large cauldron appeared next to him. Red flames burst from it.

The priest faced the crowd. "We begin The Blessing to both bring luck to the competitors and to tie them to the Battle of Heirs. There is no backing out from this point forward."

Cade's expression didn't change. Raith straightened his head.

The priest continued. "As winner of The Hunt, Raith has first choice for his second."

Second? Second what?

Raith glanced at Cade, a smirk forming on his face. "I select *Scarlett*."

"No," Cade said. "You can't."

The priest looked between the two brothers. "Is there a problem?"

"Scarlett is *my* human," Cade said.

"No," Raith said. "You wish she was yours. She has not bound herself to you."

Cade's gaze burned into Raith.

"Then she is available," the priest said. "But a human for your second? Are you sure?"

"Yep."

Satisfaction burst from Raith, wrath from Cade. Raith's gaze found Scarlett as his brother glared at him with a venomous stare.

Now she wished she *hadn't* come to The Blessing. Not

that it would have changed anything, but at least she wouldn't have everyone turn to stare at her like they were doing now.

"Will Scarlett please come up to the balcony?" the priest asked.

Scarlett wasn't sure what was going on, but she did as she was asked. The crowd parted as she made her way to the stairs, her heels clinking with each step up, murmurs echoing behind her.

Fury cloaked Cade's face as Scarlett approached. Raith wore a triumphant expression. Had this been his plan all along?

"To deny a second request is treason," the priest said as he stared at Scarlett. "You will be in the Battle of Heirs as Raith's partner. Either Cade or his second can kill you and you them. Should Cade defeat Raith or Raith surrender, your fate will be up to Cade."

Well, that sucked. She was supposed to fight in a fae battle? But she was human—well, maybe she wasn't. But the only thing she'd been able to do so far is sense emotion and heal Abigail, neither of which compared to what Raith and Cade could do.

"You may stand next to Raith," the priest said.

Scarlett moved next to him, avoiding Cade's eyes. Would he hate her now? Did it even matter if he did? Raith could take her pain away, too. But she didn't trust Raith. Then again, she didn't trust Cade either.

"Name your second, Cade," the priest said.

"Poppy," Cade said, his expression blank.

Cade's trainer stomped up the stairs. Unlike most of

the fae women in the crowd who wore dresses, she was in leather pants and a vest, as if she were ready to step into battle right now. Did she know Cade was going to choose her? The annoyance on her face told Scarlett no.

The priest repeated the rules to Poppy, her jaw clenched.

"Raith and Scarlett will be first. Please come to me." The priest stood behind the cauldron, facing the crowd. "Hold out your hands."

Raith raised his arms in front of himself, wrists pressed together. Scarlett did the same. Nervousness swam through her veins. What had she gotten herself into?

A rope of pearls appeared in the priest's hands. He wrapped them around Raith's wrists and then Scarlett's. "Place your hands over the fire."

But that would burn her! She waited for him to say he was kidding, but he didn't. She felt her fear leeched from her. Was Raith doing it?

Raith moved toward the cauldron. Tied together, Scarlett had no choice but to follow. She held her breath as her hands hit the flames. No pain. Instead, it tickled her skin. The flames turned from red to pink to purple to blue as the pearls tying them together burned away.

When they pulled their arms away from the fire, Scarlett was hit with a feeling of delight—not her own, but Raith's. She'd felt moments of emotions from others— usually from humans—but this was different.

Raith reached around Scarlett's waist and guided her away from the cauldron. It was Cade and Poppy's turn. As

Cade stepped to the priest, he shot a dagger of a glare at Raith. Raith winked in return.

Poppy didn't say a word as the rope wrapped around her wrists and then burned away. Her eyes avoided Cade completely.

Scarlett had forgotten about Kassandra. When she made the mistake of looking in the queen's direction, she was met with a snarl. Scarlett snapped her gaze away. It wasn't like she chose to be Raith's second. It was basically a death sentence as it was, but now that she was on Kassandra's bad side, she had little hope to ever make it home. Unless Raith won. Then he would be king and could offer her protection.

But if he wanted to win, why in the hell did he choose Scarlett as his second?

As the priest spoke the actual blessing, Raith stared at his brother.

The rage on Cade's face sent satisfaction coursing through Raith. His plan had worked perfectly. He didn't know he'd win The Hunt when he made the bargain with Scarlett, but he knew he had a good chance. Hunting would require a bow and arrow, and he knew Cade had never liked the weapon. When he found out about the whole removing their mind shield part he got nervous, but when he saw Theo, his confidence rose again. Then he won and had been waiting for this moment ever since.

And as much joy his brother's anger brought him, he

also planned to get Scarlett out of Cade's grasp. He sucked the poor girl dry every day. Raith didn't blame him, her emotion was tasty, but Raith had grown somewhat fond of the human.

Only, he wasn't so sure she *was* a human. Something was different about her. He knew that when she didn't die from the banshee bite. And there had to be a reason her emotion was so succulent.

When The Blessing was over, the priest excused everyone. Raith linked his arm with Scarlett and led her away from the balcony. It tingled where their skin touched. Thanks to The Blessing, they were connected now. Any chemistry they had before would only be heightened. Once they reached the hallway in front of the library doors, Raith felt something hit his back.

He turned to see Cade with a ball of summer magic in his hand.

"That could be grounds for forfeit, brother," Raith said. "No fighting before the battle. And I thought you were a rule follower."

Magic glowed in Cade's hands.

"Seriously, Cade," Poppy said as she stood next to him. "Calm the fuck down."

"Why her?" Cade asked. "I know you've never wanted to be king but a human as your second?"

"Is that concern in your voice?" Raith asked. He'd seen his brother grow attached to Scarlett. At first, he thought Cade had lost his mind, but Raith now saw her lure—which made taking her away from Cade even more gratifying

Raith glanced at Scarlett. Her blue eyes were wide as she bit her lip. Her dark brown hair contrasted against her pale skin, freckles sprinkled across her nose. It wasn't just her beauty that drew Raith in. Even when her emotion ran low after Cade's feedings, Scarlett had spunk.

Right then, nervousness emanated from her, along with relief. The bond of The Blessing had strengthened Raith's connection to her.

Whenever Raith visited the mortal world, humans annoyed him more than anything. But Scarlett was different than most humans.

"She is *mine*," Cade said.

"No, she's not," Raith said. "She's no one's. But she's linked to me now whether you like it or not."

Cade swung his arm back, summer magic still burning in his hand.

"Now hold on," Raith said. "We can make a deal."

Poppy reached for Cade's arm and pulled it to his side. She gritted her teeth. "Don't be an idiot."

"What kind of deal?" Cade asked.

"If Scarlett agrees, she can stay with you until the battle, except for a training session and strategy meeting with me every day to prepare. You cannot force her, with or without your gifts, to do anything, and you cannot feed from her emotion."

How much would Scarlett mean to Cade if she weren't a power source?

"Fine."

"Let's shake on it." Raith stuck out his right hand.

Straight faced, Cade gripped Raith's hand and they

shook. It was done. Should Cade break the bargain, he'd be cursed. Sometimes a broken promise could end in madness, other times a loss of magic, now and again death—never anything good.

Cade wasn't an idiot. He'd follow through with the agreement, but Raith hoped the struggle would distract him. It was part of his strategy. And he was banking on the fact that Scarlett wasn't entirely human. But even if she was, he doubted Cade would hurt her in the battle. His brother had always been the chivalrous one.

Raith suspected Poppy, on the other hand, would have no problem sticking a sword through Scarlett's chest. But she would be under Cade's command.

"We're leaving." Cade motioned for Scarlett to come to him. She did, but on the way her eyes met Raith's and he felt her confliction. He almost regretted making the bargain with Cade. He could have demanded she come with him and there wouldn't have been much Cade could have done to stop him. But pissing off Cade was too fun, and Scarlett wouldn't be forced to do anything she didn't want to. Most importantly, Cade would no longer drain her.

"Night, night." Raith waved as Cade guided Scarlett down the hall without so much as a goodbye to Poppy. "Picks you as his second and still walks away with the human."

"What game are you playing?" Poppy asked.

Raith leaned against the hall wall. "Whatever do you mean?"

"You're just going to get the poor girl killed."

"You care about the mortal, too? How cute."

"I don't think humans should get caught up in fae politics." Poppy crossed her arms. "Now I'm off to get a good night's sleep since apparently *I'm* being dragged into fae politics."

"Sleep tight."

❧

BACK IN HIS ROOM, Cade removed his shirt and chucked it across his room. God he hated his brother. Raith was always a thorn in Cade's side, but now that thorn had morphed into a knife and jabbed Cade straight in the back.

Technically, Scarlett wasn't Cade's. She hadn't given her allegiance to him or agreed to stay in Faerie under him for an agreed amount of time. But Cade found her and she *should* be his. Now she was bonded with Raith. Cade kicked the corner of his bed.

Scarlett had said goodnight and left to take a bath, likely still in shock from everything that had happened. A human in a Battle of Heirs. It was unheard of. She had every right to be scared out of her mind. Humans were weak and frail.

Cade tried to sleep but couldn't. The anger coursing through his body energized him. Instead, he closed his eyes and thought of Scarlett.

When he entered her dreamscape, she was walking around the castle gardens, smelling a rose. The sun shone brightly overhead in a cloudless sky. Cade thought of dark clouds rolling in and so they did, pushing away the warmth of the sun.

Rain poured down in huge drops. Scarlett ran toward the front of the castle, but Cade put up an iron fence blocking her way.

Then a creature stepped out from behind a bush—a banshee. That wasn't from Cade. It must have been the conjuring of Scarlett's own subconscious. But when had she seen a banshee?

The banshee stalked toward Scarlett, fangs exposed. "I told you we'd meet again."

"Leave me alone," Scarlett shouted.

"And why would I do a thing like that?" the banshee said. "You're the one who doesn't belong here. This isn't your world."

"I'll…I'll leave." Scarlett backed as far as she could until she was pressed into the wall of the castle.

"But you can't."

Scarlett glanced to her wrists, a purple outline of the blessing rope tattooed to her skin.

Cade moved back into his own mind. The dream should be far enough along for his plan to work, a big thanks to Scarlett's own fear. Cade went to Scarlett's room. She was asleep in her bed, body curled into the fetal position.

He shook her gently. "Scarlett, wake up."

When she awoke, she jumped at the sight of Cade.

"It's okay," Cade said. "You were having a bad dream."

He could feel her fear, but he couldn't feed off of her

emotion, so he let it be. There were other ways for him to recharge his power.

"Come here," he pulled her into an embrace and brushed the hair out of her face. "You're okay."

Her body sank into his as she sobbed. "I'm going to die."

"Shh…" He rubbed her back. "No, you're not."

It might be a lie. Cade and Poppy wouldn't be the only dangerous things in the battle.

Cade placed a finger under her chin and lifted her face. He gently pressed his lips onto hers. At first, she merely accepted the kiss, but then her lips kissed back. He lifted Scarlett and lowered her onto the bed and moved on top of her.

Scarlett's breathing grew heavy. Cade could hear her heartbeat race. He took in the passion between them. The bargain kept him from feeding on her emotion, but Raith didn't mention anything about sex not being allowed.

Since Scarlett's pain had been so strong, Cade had never seduced her all the way. But now the power in him roared. If Raith thought he could stop Scarlett from helping Cade win the battle, he was wrong.

Chapter Twenty-Four

A moan escaped Scarlett's lips as Cade lifted her silky nightgown and brushed his fingers against her stomach. His warm touch soothed her, pulling her from the lingering darkness of her dream. When his finger hooked the waistband of her panties, Scarlett froze.

What was she doing?

He'd awoken her from that nightmare and then was kissing her and it felt good. She didn't know if she'd live past the battle, and his lips on her neck helped dull her fear.

"No, stop." Scarlett panted as she tried to rein the thoughts exploding through her brain like fireworks.

Cade's lips touched her neck again and he jolted back, pressing his hand to his mouth. "What the..."

The bargain said Scarlett couldn't be forced to do anything against her will. Somehow, its magic must have stopped him.

"I'm sorry," Scarlett said.

Why was she apologizing? She didn't want to sleep with him. So what? She didn't owe him anything.

"What's the matter?" he asked, his voice gentle.

"I just don't feel like doing this."

His eyes narrowed. "Typical human."

"Excuse me?"

"You don't appreciate everything I've done for you. You'd be sitting on top of that hill still mourning if it weren't for me. What kind of life was that?"

"It was *my* life, and I would have figured it out eventually." Anger boiled inside Scarlett. She pulled her nighty back into place.

"Pfff." Cade got up from her bed and headed to the door, leaving without another word.

What an ass. He'd only been using her for the power she gave him, which, if Scarlett was being honest, she'd known all along. He hadn't brought her here to save her. He'd lured her into his world for his own gain. If she couldn't help him anymore, she was useless to him. But he was right; she was weak. Running away was easier than facing it all, so that's what she did—all the way to another realm.

She'd dug her own grave, but maybe, just maybe, there was a way to escape it.

Chapter Twenty-Five

A lmost as if his feet had minds of their own, Raith walked down the unfamiliar path to the infirmary. There had been no war during his lifetime, and since the fae rarely got sick, he'd had no reason to come to this part of the castle.

Except once.

He and Cade had snuck into the battle wing after their classes one day. Their father had told them a million times to stay away until they were old enough to start training, which only fueled their curiosity. Raith was twelve, Cade seven. It would be three years until Raith was old enough to train. He only wanted to see what the battle wing was like. They'd be careful.

"We're going to get in trouble," Cade said as they made it into a room full of weapons. He was always afraid of being caught somewhere he shouldn't be.

Raith, on the other hand, enjoyed the thrill of breaking the rules.

"Not if you keep quiet." Raith admired a set of daggers hanging on the wall. "These are amazing."

Cade glanced over Raith's shoulder. "Whoa. Real weapons."

"Here, let's fight." Raith tossed one of the daggers at Cade's feet.

Cade picked it up and twirled it in his hands. "We shouldn't."

Raith struck his dagger, making contact with Cade's.

Cade didn't swing back.

"Don't be a baby," Raith said. "Fight."

Cade raised his dagger and gave a half-hearted swing at Raith. "This isn't a good idea. Mother wouldn't like it."

His mom wouldn't like it. Kassandra was not Raith's mother. "Awww, momma's boy, are you?"

"Shut up," Cade said.

"Does she still rock you to sleep at night?" Raith hit Cade's dagger again.

"Stop."

"Gonna go cry to mommy?"

"I said stop!" Cade screamed as he sliced his dagger at Raith's face, the orb on the dagger's handle glowing green.

Raith lunged backwards as the dagger came toward his eye, scraping the top of his eyebrow. "Ow."

"I'm sorry." Cade dropped his dagger and stepped to Raith.

"Get away."

Even with Raith's enhanced healing power as a fae, the wound wouldn't close. He would have to tell his father what happened. As he pressed his sleeve into the cut, he saw the panic on Cade's face. So, when he found his father, he lied. He told him he snuck in alone and was throwing the dagger in the air when it came down and sliced him. His father gave him a long stare, but said the cut was punishment enough.

Raith had to go to the infirmary to have a nurse look at his wound. She told the king that it had been done with a blade enhanced with summer magic. She could make the bleeding stop but there may still be a small scar.

Raith hadn't been back since, but the nurse had been right, the scar still remained.

When he opened the infirmary door, a nurse looked up. Her expression softened when she recognized Raith. "The king is at the end, behind the curtain."

It was the same nurse who had fixed his eye—the best she could, at least.

Raith nervously walked to the king.

His father looked frail lying on the bed, his legs tucked underneath blankets. His gray hair nearly reached his shoulders now—a big change to the neatly trimmed cut he wore when Raith was a child.

The king opened his eyes. A smile formed on his face. "My son."

Raith magicked a chair from across the room next to the bed and sat down. He took his father's hand into his own. "What's happened to you?"

His father coughed. "She's consumed my mind."

"Kassandra?"

The king shook his head. "Your mother."

Raith didn't know what to say, so he kept silent.

His father continued, "I see her in my dreams and when I'm awake. She haunts me constantly. I watch her scream in pain, watch her die. And then she returns."

Ghosts weren't real. His mother had died long ago. She was gone.

"I miss her more than anything." The king squeezed Raith's hand.

Raith held in the tears forming behind his eyes. He wouldn't cry. Not now.

"Would you like to see her?" his father asked.

"She's gone, father."

"No, son. In my mind. The good times, not the bad."

Raith nodded and closed his eyes.

He dove into his father's mind.

❧❧❧

THE KING RODE through the dark forest on a gray mare. The smell of pine enveloped him. He'd always loved to ride but rarely ventured far from the castle. His father always discouraged it.

But now—his father was gone and the king could do what he pleased. His horse picked up speed, gracefully galloping through the thicket of the trees.

Why had his father been so fearful of the woods? It was lovely here. He slowed the horse down and hopped off, tying her to a tree by a creek. As the horse drank, the king explored. Twigs crunched beneath his feet as he wove a path through the trees. A note was stuck to one of the trunks.

He meandered to it, paying no attention to his footing. As he reached for the note, a rope strangled his ankles and sent him flying upward, feet first. His crown clunked to the ground. He struggled, but something tied a chain around his wrists. The king tried to use his magic to free his feet, but his magic didn't work.

"Gotchya." A short creature with long, pointed ears and ash brown skin looked the upside-down king face-to-face.

A goblin.

It bent down and picked up the crown from the ground, inspecting it carefully with its long, thin fingers. It bit down on the metal.

"Let me go," the king demanded.

The goblin laughed. "You have no room to bargain here, *King*."

He was in trouble. Of all the stupid things to do, getting caught by a goblin was high on the list. Goblins were nasty creatures, greedy to their core.

An arrow flew through the air, missing the king's face by two inches. The goblin cocked its head around. A woman, with long, mahogany hair approached them.

"Next time, I won't miss, goblin."

The goblin snarled at the woman, but it dropped the crown and scurried away into the woods.

The woman glanced at the crown and then to the king. "A Summer Court fae, caught by a goblin of all things." The woman laughed, propping her bow against a tree. With a wave of her hand, the rope at the king's feet untied and he dropped to the ground with a thud. She bent down and pulled the chains off of his wrist.

He had never seen a more spectacular woman. The life in her eyes shined like a comet in the night's sky.

Whoever she was, he wanted to get to know her better.

❧

RAITH PULLED BACK into his own mind. A tear dripped down his father's cheek. Raith choked back his own emotion.

"I loved her," the king said. "So much."

"Me too," Raith said.

"I'm sorry I wasn't a good father to you."

Raith shrugged. "You could have done better. But you weren't all bad." He wouldn't sugar coat it. The older Raith got, the more distant his father became. But they'd had good times. That's what made it hurt.

A coughing fit attacked the king. He closed his eyes and rested his head on his pillow.

"I'll let you rest." Raith gave his father's hand one last squeeze.

He was already late for his training session with Scarlett. He hadn't planned to visit his father, but he was glad he did. Seeing his mother through the king's eyes brought both happiness and anger to Raith. At one time, they were truly in love. And then his mother died and everything was ruined.

As a child, he believed everyone was wrong. He hadn't

been allowed to see her body in the casket and he'd convinced himself it meant it was only a trick; she wasn't really dead. But as the days and nights passed, his theory grew weaker, until one day, he knew it has been a silly wish.

The pain of losing her eased little by little, but so did his hopeful spirit. His life sucked. That was the reality. When Kassandra came along, everything got worse.

Raith shifted his thoughts to the battle as he climbed the stairs in the training tower. Jaser and Scarlett were talking when Raith entered the battle room.

"And he honors us with his presence," Jaser said. "Scarlett and I were just getting to know each other a little better while we waited for your late ass."

"I'm here now, aren't I?"

"My, my, someone woke up on the wrong side of the bed," Jaser said.

Scarlett just stared at Raith. Thanks to the blessing bond, he knew she could sense his mood. He could feel her concern for him, mixed with her own turmoil.

"Let's get started," Raith said.

Chapter Twenty-Six

S carlett sensed Raith's bad mood the moment he entered the room. Even before she could see him, she felt something was off. Ever since she'd entered Faerie, things had felt different. She'd sensed the emotion of others on multiple occasions, but this was something *else*. Something stronger. It was as if Raith's mood was her mood, too. Like they were connected, two parts of a whole.

"Okay, time to teach the mortal to fight," Jaser said. "This should be fun."

When Scarlett first saw Jaser, she nearly ran the other way. He had a fierceness to him that intimidated her. Then he said, "Hey, human."

She relaxed. Something about his nonchalance assured her he was okay. A nice change to the stares of all the other fae.

Now that Raith was there, they began training.

"So, what combat experience do you have?" Jaser asked Scarlett.

"Um, none." Unless they counted the fistfight she got into in third grade because a bully made fun of Natalie's haircut. The cut was awful, but that didn't give him the right to embarrass her, so Scarlett tackled him on the playground. She was clearly winning when a teacher pulled them apart and she got suspended for three days. Her mom was *not* very happy when she picked her up from school, but when Scarlett told her why she got in the fight, she lightened up. Thankfully, she'd been on her medication then. Otherwise, who knew how she would have reacted.

"Okay, so a beginner." Jaser turned to the wall of weapons. "Let's start with a staff." He pulled it from the wall and chucked it to Scarlett.

She caught it.

"She can catch, that's a start," Jaser joked.

It was a simple wooden staff. Scarlett held it awkwardly, not sure what she should do.

Jaser grabbed a fancier looking staff from the wall. It was metal with a white orb in its center. When he gripped the staff, the orb lit up orange, powered with fae magic like Cade had showed her before. "Step one, hold it firmly in front of yourself."

Scarlett did as he said. He hit his staff with hers. Her staff flinched toward her, but only a little.

"Good." Jaser swung again, this time lower.

Scarlett moved the staff to meet his hit.

Jaser looked at Raith. "Well, if you're going to have a

human as your second, this one has good reflexes." He winked at Scarlett.

Jaser refereed to Scarlett as a *human*, but there was no malice to the tone of his tongue. Both Cade and Raith had treated Scarlett like she was more than something to be spit on, which was the vibe she got from the other fae in Faerie, but the brothers seemed possessive of her. Jaser's attitude toward her was different—like she was a friend.

Jaser continued, "Since we only have a week to prepare, I think we should stick to the staff. It will be less threatening to Cade and Poppy, so they'll feel less pressure to kill you."

"That's a plus," Scarlett said, half-seriously, half-jokingly.

"I agree," Raith said. It was the first thing he'd said in a while. Scarlett felt sadness from the bond. Something was on his mind. Either Jaser didn't notice, or didn't care, because his focus was solely on Scarlett.

Jaser continued to show Scarlett defensive moves with the staff—how to block from one attack to the next. Even she was pleasantly surprised at how well she defended herself. She was sure Jaser was going easy on her, but still. She was far better at it than she could have hoped for.

"Okay, now you take this one, and I'll grab a sword," Jaser said. "It has fae magic in it which won't do you much good, but a wooden one would do a piss poor job against a blade. The fae magic makes the blows more lethal, preventing fae healing ability from working."

Scarlett switched staffs. She wondered if anything, would happen when she gripped the metal staff as it had when she touched the dagger the day she'd been there with Cade. As soon as her skin touched it, the orb glowed purple.

"What in the hell?" Jaser said. "Raith, look."

Raith glanced at the staff in Scarlett's hand. "Well, look at that."

"What?" Scarlett asked. She had been careful not to let Cade see her touch the dagger that day—in case it meant something, which, apparently, it did. Somehow, Raith didn't seem surprised.

"Did you know?" Jaser asked Raith.

"I had a hunch."

"How?"

And they were both ignoring Scarlett's question. Great.

"Come here, Scarlett," Raith said.

She went to him. He placed his hands on the side of her head and closed his eyes. Then a memory came flooding into Scarlett's mind—when she got bit by the banshee and Raith saved her. He took her to his tree house and then back to her room and erased her memory. It wasn't her memory, but his.

"You messed with my head," she said.

"I'm sorry," Raith said. "Truly. I don't like to do that to people. I just didn't want you knowing it was me who saved you, at least not then."

If she couldn't feel the bond between them, she may have thought he was lying and didn't care at all about what he'd done. But regret trickled from him and Scarlett couldn't find it in herself to be mad about it. Everything in life had gotten so screwed up, having a memory stolen barely registered on the scale of her problems.

Raith told Jaser how the banshee bit Scarlett and he couldn't find any serum to heal its poison, so he thought Scarlett would die. But she didn't.

"What does it all mean?" Scarlett asked.

"You have fae blood in you," Raith said.

Scarlett remembered her healing powers. It all made sense. Yet, how could it be?

She thought long and hard for a moment—should she tell them about her ability to heal or not? She hated to get even more wrapped up in this world than she already was, but if she and Raith didn't win the battle, she could die.

What choice did she have but to trust them?

"Let me show you something," Scarlett said. "Do you have a blade that isn't made with fae magic?"

Jaser gave her a small knife. "This work?"

"Yes." Scarlett took the blade and asked Raith for his hand. "I need to cut you."

Raith nodded, eyebrow raised. The blade was sharp and his skin sliced easily. He winced slightly as a wound appeared on his hand. Scarlett felt his pain through the bond.

She covered the wound with her hand and reached inside herself to heal it. She searched for the magic supply inside her, still full from her night with Cade and the sadness she'd absorbed from Raith since he'd entered the training room. She focused on the slice, feeling the break in the skin. Energy flowed from her into where the knife had pierced him. When she moved her hand, the cut was gone.

Raith inspected his hand. "I would have healed on my own from that small of a cut," he said. "But not that quickly. How did you do that?"

"I'm not sure," Scarlett said. "Kassandra stabbed one of the servants with a spoon and when I pulled it out of her, I just knew I could fix it."

Had she not seen the magic the fae possessed or felt the change in herself when she stepped into Faerie, she'd be certain she was losing her mind. What would she have thought if her mom told her that *she* could heal someone? Scarlett would have done everything she could to convince her to take her medication. But her mom never claimed any special powers. Chances were, she was mentally ill.

But Scarlett wasn't. She was *fae*—well, part fae, at least.

"She's got to be part Seelie," Jaser said. "That's crazy. They aren't supposed to mate with humans."

"We all know how well fae follow that rule," Raith replied.

"But the high and mighty Seelies are supposed to be *perfect*."

"Hello? Can you fill me in?" Scarlett waved her hands back and forth. She was the one who just found out she was partly some supernatural creature she hadn't even known about until a few months ago.

"The Seelie and Unseelie like to think of themselves as the elite fae. Seelies are supposed to be the lighter fae, the Unseelie the darker. A few decades ago, to show their superiority, the Seelie Queen banned her court from commingling with mortals. Looks like someone didn't listen," Jaser said.

"How does it help us in the battle?" Scarlett asked.

"Well, I don't think anyone else knows," Raith said. "So we'll have the element of surprise. And you should be stronger and faster than a regular human."

Scarlett was always quicker than the other girls, and a lot of the boys, too. She never thought much of it until now. And the ease of taking down the bully on the playground that time *was* remarkable. He was a lot bigger than she was and she tackled him like it was nothing.

"That should be enough for today," Jaser said. "We'll see what we can figure out about your power tomorrow."

Scarlett hung the staff back on the wall—the purple in the orb fading when it left her hands.

Raith walked Scarlett to her room. As he left her there alone, he said. "Don't let Cade know."

Scarlett had kept it from him this long, so what was another week? It ended up being especially easy that night because Cade didn't come to her room before she fell asleep like he normally did. She tried desperately to fall asleep, but her thoughts were too busy—her mother's death, Ashleigh's harsh words, her time in Faerie, and now the battle—everything swarmed her, making sleep impossible.

At first, she thought she had a grip on it all. She focused on her breathing, trying to clear her mind. It didn't work. She felt the pain and panic grow and swirl together inside her chest. She needed to get it under control. If only she knew how.

Scarlett felt trapped in this room. She'd spent too much time in it, waiting for Cade to arrive and take away her pain. He wasn't coming tonight, and even if he did, the bargain prevented him from feeding from her emotion. Her pain was hers alone now. She needed out.

Still in her nightgown, the cold stone floor sent a chill up her leg as her bare feet pounded against it. She needed air to think. Getting away from her human troubles seemed like such a good idea. Now, she felt lost. She went out the castle backdoor without anyone noticing.

The moonlight lit the garden. Out there, the fresh air relaxed her. She breathed deeply, inhaling the scent of the rose bushes she stood next to.

"It's awfully late for a lady to be outside alone." Raith whispered behind Scarlett, his breath on her neck causing a quiver.

"I'm not a typical lady." Scarlett turned. Raith towered above her. His steel blue eyes glistened in the moonlight.

He placed a hand on her back. "I never thought you were."

"Cade wouldn't like us out here alone. It isn't part of the bargain." Scarlett didn't care what Cade thought, but she wondered if Raith feared his younger brother enough to leave her alone. After choosing her for his second, her guess was no.

Raith pulled Scarlett closer. "All the more reason for us to be here."

This was dangerous. Scarlett knew from the tingle in her stomach that she was tempting herself, being there with Raith. The pain she felt lingered in her bones. The memory of her mother's lifeless eyes. The coldness of her hand when Scarlett finally let go when the paramedics arrived. Everything she'd come here to escape had been hurled at her at once. Running from it lasted for a while, but that luxury had vanished. She could feel grief coming from Raith, too. Was it just the bond that let her into his head or was it part of her fae ancestry? She'd felt the emotion of the servant girl, and at times she thought she might have even known what Cade was feeling.

"You told me you can take my pain away better than Cade could," Scarlett said.

"I did."

"By taking my memories?"

"Yes."

Scarlett leaned into Raith. He could make the anguish inside her stop. Scarlett's heart raced. He could take her memories. How could something hurt her if she didn't remember it? "Away forever?"

Raith nodded. "If you want them gone forever."

Is that what Scarlett wanted? She thought about her mother's gentle touch. Her laugh. The way her eyes squinted together when she smiled. The happy memories hurt as much as the bad ones, reminding Scarlett of what she'd never have again. Most of all, a part of her now wondered if her mother hadn't been crazy. What if Scarlett had believed her?

"Do it."

Chapter Twenty-Seven

"Let's go somewhere else. To my tree house. No one will bother us there," Raith said.

Scarlett followed him. Raith had come to the gardens to clear his own head. His father's memories played on repeat in his head ever since he saw them. He'd had his mother for less than five years of his life, but even in that short amount of time, he learned what love was. His own memories of her were blurry. But his father's memories—they were as clear as glass.

When they entered his tree house, he lit the fire with his magic.

"Are you sure about this?" he asked Scarlett.

Her face was pale, her eyes wide. "I need to be focused. It's our only chance. And thinking of her hurts too much right now."

Raith moved his hands to Scarlett's face. His thumbs brushed her temples. He'd only taken away memories a few times. It always felt wrong, a violation. No one had ever asked him to do it.

She looked at him with hopeful blue eyes. With a deep breath, he peered into her mind.

A woman with a long auburn braid appeared. She pushed a young Scarlett on a swing at playground. What a silly thing humans did, but both the woman and Scarlett looked happy. He could feel Scarlett's happiness in the memory. The safety she felt. The feeling of being loved.

He couldn't do it.

It would be so easy to erase Scarlett's memories. It would fuel him up for the upcoming battle. Probably even piss Cade off more. But he thought of the few memories he had of his own mother and the joy Scarlett felt with hers. He couldn't take that from her.

What a great time for him to get sentimental.

"I can't," he said.

He felt relief shoot from her. But he also felt her pain. She'd lost her favorite person in the whole world, just as he did. And while hers was fresher than his, he'd pent up all his feelings for so long, he felt like he might burst.

Scarlett reached up on her tiptoes and kissed Raith's mouth. The kiss sent fire through his veins. He reached around her and pulled her body into his as their mouths moved together. Her tongue grazed his as his hands moved to her hair. Neither spoke as their bodies moved together as if this were as natural as breathing. Their pain disappeared, bulldozed by passion.

He lifted Scarlett and dropped her on his bed. Hastily, she unbuttoned his pants. Raith pushed all thoughts out as he let his fervor control him. He'd never made love to a human before—then again, Scarlett wasn't fully human. He pulled her nightgown over her head. If this was a bad idea, he'd worry about it tomorrow. Everything felt too *right* to stop now.

Chapter Twenty-Eight

Scarlett's breath fluttered as Raith's hands explored her naked body. She gasped when they teasingly grazed the lowest part of her stomach.

Raith paused. Uncertainty flickered from him through the bond. Desire swam through Scarlett. Raith continued to roam Scarlett's flesh with his fingertips.

When he stopped, lust flooded Scarlett. Her eyes met his and he grinned deviously. He pushed himself on top of her and leaned his face toward her.

Scarlett had waited this long to make love to someone —turned down guy after guy she'd dated. It was never to protect her virginity as some sacred piece of her. But it had always felt *wrong* when things would go too far. She'd always found the will to stop.

Not now.

She wanted this more than she'd wanted anything.

Raith's mouth crashed into hers. There was no uncertainty from the bond now. Passion exploded from both of them. Scarlett's hands travelled across Raith's chest, down the curves of his abs, then lower. He moaned.

His body was almost flawless. She looked into his eyes, glancing at the scar above his eyebrow. It was the one blemish that made him seem real. He wasn't perfect. Like her, he'd experienced deep pain. It connected them as much as the ritual that created the bond between them had.

Doubt vanished from Scarlett's mind. Only this moment mattered. Her fervor consumed her as her body took control. Scarlett and Raith became yearning incarnate. Their mouths roamed each other's bodies, discovering the most sensitive parts.

Time slowed as they took their time. Scarlett's back arched as his mouth nibbled on her earlobe. His finger found other delicate places. The magic inside her pulsed as she consumed his lust.

Raith's hands held her head as he pressed his lips to hers again. When he pulled back, their eyes met.

Neither spoke, but their gazes said enough. They understood each other. Nothing before or after this moment mattered. There was no promise in the passion between them. It was untamed and reckless and true.

Tangled skin to skin, they fell asleep together, and, for now, that moment was all that mattered.

SCARLETT AWOKE, her naked body twined with Raith's.

Last night had been a frenzy. Pain turned to lust, and all of Scarlett's worries had vanished in the moment.

Something about it had been pure.

But now Scarlett didn't know how to feel. She needed to get back to her room before Cade noticed she was missing. For all she knew, he was done with her. Her emotion was of no use to him now. But she wasn't sure and the last thing she needed was for things to get more complicated.

As passionate as last night had been, it complicated things. So much. But she could worry about that later, when she was back in her room.

Raith slept next to her, messy hair and closed eyes. He wore a peaceful expression. Scarlett had felt an assortment of emotions from the bond, but never the lull that filled it now. It almost felt criminal to disturb him. But she didn't want Cade looking for her and, heaven forbid, finding her with Raith.

She shook Raith's arm to stir him awake. When his eyes opened, contentment pulsed from the bond.

"I need to get back to my room…unnoticed," Scarlett said.

They both got dressed in silence. Scarlett wondered what thoughts crossed Raith's mind. She was the one who kissed him first. God, what was she thinking? That was the problem—she wasn't. When he wouldn't take her memories, both terror and relief bombarded her. She didn't want to forget her mother, but she didn't want to feel everything anymore. Instead of worrying about her conflicting emotions, Scarlett acted out of instinct.

"I can get you in through the back door. I'd evanesce

you in, but my brother could be waiting for you in your room." Raith said as they walked around the castle grounds.

The sun was just rising, the sky still pale. Sunrise promised a new beginning. Scarlett inhaled the freshness of the new day.

"I thought it was an exit only door?" she asked.

"It is, unless you're royalty. Then the door will open."

"Oh."

When they arrived at the door, they stood awkwardly, gazes locked.

What should Scarlett say? She didn't regret their night together—but she had no idea what it meant. A one night stand in the moment? Somehow, it felt bigger than that. Yet, neither of them knew what would happen during the battle. Preparing for it needed to be the focus—not whatever was or wasn't between them.

"I'll see you at training later," Raith said.

"See you then." Scarlett hurried inside before either could say anything else.

When she was back in her room, she fell back on her bed, sinking into the mattress. Had she actually asked Raith to take her memories? What had gotten into her? Those memories were all she had left of her mom. Without them, who would she be?

Her mother didn't raise her to be so fragile. Her mom taught her to be strong. To fight when life had you down —until she killed herself, that was. But that was the sickness, not her mom. And here Scarlett was, trapped in the fae world because she was too scared to face it all. If Raith had done as she asked, Scarlett would have lost her mother forever.

Scarlett closed her eyes and released her fear. When she opened them, a new determination swam through her. She would fight until the end.

A knock at the door startled her.

It was Peony. "The Queen has called an announcement and asked that everyone in the castle meet in the ballroom."

Scarlett dressed quickly into a clean outfit and made her way to the ballroom. The room was full of the castle staff. Cade and Kassandra stood on the balcony. Raith stood in the back corner of the room behind everyone. Why wasn't he with Kassandra and Cade?

"Welcome," Kassandra said. "I have unfortunate news. I'm afraid the king has perished."

A murmur swept through the crowd. A punch of sadness hit Scarlett—not her own, but Raith's. He always seemed to distance himself from the king, but the king was his father. Losing him couldn't be easy.

"Since the Battle of Heirs has already begun, I will step up as interim ruler," Kassandra added.

The pain coming from Raith turned to anger. Fury punched her.

"Fae from all over the Summer Court, as well as important guests from the other courts, will be coming to witness the battle. I expect the castle to be in perfect condition. Anyone who does anything less will answer to me."

Fear swept through the room.

"That's all," Kassandra said. "Back to work."

Scarlett looked for Raith, but he was already gone. She could still feel rage coming from the bond, but with Raith out of her sight, it wasn't as strong.

When Scarlett went to her training session, Jaser was the only one there.

"Hello, mortal-fae." Jaser grinned. "Raith is taking a day off, so it's just us."

They got straight to work. Today, Jaser showed her what summer energy was. It was basically a ball of light in his hands that he could hurl at someone.

"Depending how powerful the blast is, it could knock you down, or with enough power behind it, shoot a hole right through you." Jaser's summer energy was orange in color. "I'm going to throw some at you."

Scarlett stared at him. "What?"

"You can block them with your staff," Jaser said. "Don't worry, they'll be weak. If they hit you, they'll sting, but they won't do any real damage."

Scarlett held her staff in front of her as Jaser stood across the room and threw balls of energy at her. Who knew years of playing softball could save her life? Swinging the staff was different than swinging a bat, but it required the same hand-eye coordination.

The key was timing. As the energy flew at her, she kept her eyes on it until the staff hit it away. Its weight was different than a bat—thinner, longer, and more evenly dispersed.

The more Jaser threw, the faster he threw them, with less and less time between each throw. After hitting nearly twenty with her staff, one got by and hit her in the leg. It burned through her leather pants.

"Ow!"

A welt appeared on her skin, stinging as the breeze from the open window hit it. Her magic supply still surged from the night before. When she thought of her leg unblemished, and the welt disappeared before her eyes.

"Nice," Jaser said. "You can heal yourself."

"Only if I'm alive to do it."

CADE BUTTONED HIS BLACK JACKET. Even though the fae were supernatural and wouldn't die of old age, when they did die, they paid their respects with a funeral, just as humans did.

The royal cemetery lay in the back corner of the castle grounds, surrounded by rose bushes and other hedges to keep it private. The High Priest stood by the white, marble casket holding the king's body.

Cade still couldn't believe his father was gone. His father was still a young king, whose own father was nearly three-hundred-years old when he was killed in the last major fae war. But the king was only eighty—still a young adult in the fae world.

Something had been wrong with him for a while. It wasn't unheard of for a fae to lose his mind—just rare. Regardless of why, the king was dead.

Cade and Kassandra stood next to the priest. Right before the ceremony began, Raith showed up, taking his place next to Cade. The castle servants were there to give their respects, too.

Everyone wore black, the proper color of mourning. Some cried. No one spoke. To do so at the ceremony so would be treasonous. Only the High Priest and family were allowed to speak. Anyone else murmuring even a single word was disrespectful.

As the High Priest gave his blessing, Cade remembered his father. The king had taught Cade about the history of the fae and how the Summer Kings before him had ruled.

When Cade won the battle—he *would* defeat Raith— he hoped to be as good a king as his father was. The Summer Court had seen true peace, and his father respected all beings, including humans. Cade admired his father's kindness.

Once the ceremony was over, Cade went back to his room to have some time alone with his thoughts. In a few days, the battle would begin. The winner would immediately be king. Cade had always expected his father to live for at least a while longer—not for the winner of the battle to become king the moment of victory. Had that ever happened before?

Truthfully, he wasn't ready to rule. He'd completed all the necessary lessons, but he'd just become an adult in the fae world. He should have studied harder. What if other courts saw his young age as weakness and attacked? What if the people didn't respect him?

He exhaled the worry he felt about the future. First, he needed to win the battle. Then he'd figure the rest out.

One of the queen's servants came to Cade's room. His mother required his presence. Cade sighed, but went straight to her room. He wasn't sure how his mother was handling his father's death. She was never one to show her emotion. But if she needed Cade for anything, he would be there.

The queen sat on a chaise by the window in her room. "Son, come, sit." She gestured to the chair next to her.

The door closed behind Cade as he walked to her.

"With the king gone, our victory is more crucial than it's ever been. Now is the time for you to focus."

"Of course, I've been training every day."

"So has Raith, and he's been strategizing. Why else would he claim the human as his second?"

"To mess with my head," Cade said. That was Raith. Always finding a way to stir the pot. But picking Scarlett as his second was sloppy and foolish. She was no match for Poppy, a trained Summer soldier. Her mortal nature made her weak and slow and breakable. Had Cade not gotten to know Scarlett, he'd be delighted at his brother's choice. But the image of Scarlett dead on the forest ground sent a twinge of sadness through him.

"I'm sure that was part of it, but he also took away your main power source," Kassandra said. "And I think you've grown fond of the human."

He'd enjoyed his time with Scarlett, sure. But he wasn't attached enough to let it interfere. More than anything, he felt sorry for her, he assured himself.

"What exactly is the bargain you made with Raith?" Kassandra asked.

"Scarlett is mine except for a training session a day with Raith, but I can't feed on her emotion or make her do anything against her will."

He hadn't had much use for her since she stopped Cade in bed. He could feel his power building from his lust, and then once she said to stop, it froze.

"She's only a burden to you now, son," Kassandra said.

"What should I do?"

"She should be put in the dungeon. It will mess with her focus, as well as show Raith she means nothing to you."

The dungeon? That had to be a little extreme. Scarlett hadn't done anything to Cade. It was all Raith. His father would never have approved. But his father wasn't there anymore.

"Even now, you're questioning if I'm right," Kassandra said. "The stakes are too high for you to show any mercy. You must be strong. For your father."

Guilt sat in the pit of Cade's stomach, but he agreed. Kassandra would have her guards take Scarlett and lock her up, only allowing her out for her training session per Cade's agreement with Raith.

Then, in a few days, Cade would take his brother down.

Chapter Twenty-Nine

❧❦❧

A hand on her wrist yanked Scarlett from her dreamscape. Her eyes snapped open. A fae soldier, dressed like the guards at the doors, pulled Scarlett from her bed. Two others joined him. Scarlett kicked as three guards dragged her from her room. Two held her arms and the last, her leg.

"Let me go," she yelled as they walked by a group of servants.

Her fighting was futile. The guards held her until they tossed her into a cell underneath the castle. Scarlett landed on her butt with a thud.

Anger radiated through her. What assholes. Had Cade asked for her to be thrown in the dungeon like some criminal? All because she turned him down? Typical.

There was a thin mattress on the floor in the corner of the cell with a blanket and a pillow. On the other end was a toilet. This was literally a prison. Scarlett screamed, but no one paid her any attention.

The stone floor sent a shiver up her back, so she moved to the bed. Eventually, she curled under the covers and tried to clear her mind.

Hours later—how many, Scarlett didn't know—Raith showed up with a guard who unlocked her cell.

"C'mon," Raith said. Scarlett could feel the rage bursting from him.

When they were in the training room, Raith exploded. "I can't believe that bitch would do this. And, of course, my little brother went along with it."

"What's going on?" Jaser asked.

"They've locked her in the dungeon." Raith gestured to Scarlett. "I honestly underestimated Cade's momma's boy syndrome."

Scarlett still hadn't spoken. Everything was spinning out of control, faster and faster with each passing moment. All she wanted was her own bed and her old life. No fae. No battles. No powers. Why had she so desperately wanted her life to be something else? Things were hard at times, but things were safe. Somehow, she'd even managed not to get thrown in prison until coming to Faerie.

"Are you okay?" Jaser came to Scarlett and placed his hands on her shoulders. "They're doing this to mess with you. The battle is in in a few days. Don't let them ruin you now."

Scarlett blinked. The world around her came into focus. Jaser peered down at her with chocolate eyes. "Why do you care? I'm just a stupid human. What do I matter to a fae like you?"

"Throwing a pity party isn't going to save you," Jaser said. "And not all fae think so little of you humans, which, by the way, you aren't one-hundred-percent. I've been to the mortal realm a few times and from what I saw, humans can be kind, generous, and loving. Sure, most fae put themselves on a pedestal and look down upon mortals, but that's not me."

Scarlett gulped back tears. Everything was so overwhelming, but she felt the sincerity behind Jaser's words and it made her want to cry. The emotional roller coaster she'd been riding had come crashing down, throwing Scarlett against the pavement of her new reality.

"Now, we have a battle to prepare for." Jaser tossed Scarlett a staff and Raith daggers. "You two can practice against each other."

She could do this. She'd spent enough time running from her problems. It was her chance to face them—all of them. Crying would not save her and neither would cowering.

Scarlett put all her anger into practice. Raith would always find a way to give the killing blow, but the more they practiced, the longer Scarlett could hold her own. At least she was improving. If she had more time, she might turn into a competent fighter. But she didn't, so she'd have to learn the best she could. Hopefully it would be enough to keep her alive. Finally, Raith said it was time to head back to her cell, otherwise the guards would find her and drag her back.

Jaser nodded, his stare full of sympathy. On the way to the dungeon, Raith pulled Scarlett into a dark room.

Raith waved his hands and the curtains flung open. Another flick and the door shut. Next to the window sat a cherry wood grand piano—the same shade as Scarlett's mother's casket.

The grief struck her, but she didn't shy away from it this time. She allowed it to flow through her like water.

"I wanted to apologize," Raith said to Scarlett's left, her eyes fixated on the piano. "I wanted to do as you asked and take your memories. I just…couldn't."

She looked to him. "Thank you."

"I'm sorry?" Confusion filled his features.

"I'm glad you didn't erase them." She looked back to the piano. A thick layer of dust covered it, but the beautiful tone of the wood still shined in sunlight. "It was wrong of me to ask you."

"Do you play?"

"Play what?"

Raith tilted his head to the piano. "You've barely glanced at anything else since we came in here."

Scarlett nodded. "I haven't touched a piano since she died."

"It was my mother's. This was her special room. She'd play for hours, looking out to the forest in between songs," Raith said. "Would you like to play?"

Scarlett's fingers shook, but she walked toward it. She brushed the dust off of the bench and sat down. She knew she might never make it home. Her fingers hovered over the keys. She ignored the dust as she pressed down a chord.

Her fingers took control of her mind as they moved to

Chopin's Waltz in B Minor. She remembered her mother's smile as she'd listen to her learn it. When the song was through, Scarlett folded her hands in her lap.

"You miss her, too." Scarlett's gaze met Raith's. "I can feel it."

"It's why I couldn't take your memories. I couldn't imagine if I forgot my mother. I couldn't take yours from you."

Raith joined Scarlett on the bench.

"I thought I'd never be able to handle them, but when I realized they could have been gone forever, I knew I needed them. Memories are all I have left of her."

Scarlett had thought she was only part of the game, but sitting here next to Raith, the connection between them vibrated.

"I'm also sorry…about what happened next." Raith stared at the floor. "I mean, it was great, but you were vulnerable."

"I knew what I was doing." Scarlett bumped her hip against his. "You seemed to know what you were doing, too."

He grinned. "You weren't too bad yourself."

Before Scarlett could ask where they stood now, the three guards who stole her from her bed barged into the room.

"Time's up," one barked.

Anger poured from Raith.

"It's fine," Scarlett said. "I'll be okay."

She hoped.

THE NEXT DAYS were all the same. Scarlett was stuck in the cold room until it was time to train. A servant would bring her three meals a day, all some gross mush that Scarlett could barely get down. The night before the battle, Raith brought her an actual meal of turkey, potatoes, and fruit. It tasted divine—almost as if she were a prisoner on death row given her last meal.

They hadn't had a chance to finish their conversation. Every moment together went toward training. If they didn't live past the battle, their feelings for each other didn't matter.

After Scarlett finished dinner, she got into her bed. As she drifted to sleep, she heard Kassandra.

"My, my, don't you look *comfortable*." Kassandra's tone was pure ice.

"What do you want?" Scarlett asked. The time for pleasantries with the queen was over.

"Now is that any way to treat a visitor?" With a wave of her hand, Kassandra unlocked the cell and stepped inside. "Stand up."

When Scarlett didn't listen, she felt her mind explode. Pain shot through her brain. Visions of her friend Natalie being stabbed plagued her. Blood oozed from Natalie's wound as her eyes became lifeless.

Then it all stopped and Scarlett's vision returned to the cell. "How did you do that?"

"It's my *gift*."

Like Cade could enter dreams and Raith could see

and take memories? Kassandra could make people see things?

Pain shot through Scarlett's head again. Instead of seeing something in her mind, her sister Ashleigh appeared in front of her, right there in the cell.

"Scarlett," Ashleigh said. "Help me."

"No!" Scarlett yelled. "Leave her alone."

"Please." Ashleigh's eyes doubled in size. She coughed. Blood dripped out of her mouth and onto the stone floor.

"Stop it!" Scarlett screamed. She tried to go to her sister, but her body was paralyzed.

Ashleigh held her stomach and vomited up more blood.

No, this couldn't be happening. Scarlett tried to look away, but her eyes were glued to the vision of her sister in front of her.

It wasn't real, Scarlett told herself. It couldn't be. Ashleigh had appeared out of nowhere. It was just a hallucination. Even knowing this didn't make it easier to watch.

A slice appeared across Ashleigh's throat, blood squirting from it like water from a hose, and she dropped to the ground.

Another spasm attacked Scarlett's mind—like a migraine but a million times worse. Scarlett pressed her fingers into her temples, but it didn't help. The pain seemed to last hours before the cell appeared in front of her again.

"My son deserves to be king. If you do anything to stop him, well, think of this as an appetizer to what I'll do to you. Next time, it won't be an illusion of your sister I kill."

Kassandra turned and left the cell, locking the door behind her.

Scarlett curled into ball on the hard stone floor and cried herself to sleep.

Chapter Thirty

Scarlett was still in the fetal position when Raith woke her the next morning. He lifted her and set her on her feet.

"What happened?" he asked as he held her upright.

Scarlett shook her head as she relived the hallucinations. They had seemed so real. And although they weren't, she knew Kassandra was beyond capable of making good on her threat. Cade knew where Scarlett lived, where Ashleigh would be when she wasn't at school.

"It's okay, don't tell me. Let's get you to your room." Raith held Scarlett by the waist and evanesced them to her room.

Could Scarlett get a message to her sister, telling her never to go home? Even if she could, there was no way Ashleigh would listen to it. Why would she? Scarlett never listened to her mom's concerns about the voices in her head.

Away from the dungeon, Scarlett could think a little clearer. "I didn't know you could do that."

"Evanesce? Most high fae can, but it takes our magic from us, so most of us don't do it often."

"Shouldn't you be saving your magic for the battle?" Scarlett stepped away from Raith. Though still weak, she was able to stand on her own now.

"I'll be fine," Raith said. "I'm going to have someone bring you breakfast. A real meal, not that garbage they were feeding you…before."

Scarlett headed straight for the tub, catching her reflection in the mirror, her ribs poking out more than normal. Her hair was a knotted, greasy mess. She hadn't bathed in days and was sure she reeked.

After she was clean and feeling more herself, Abigail brought her breakfast.

"I'm here to help you prepare," Abigail said as she set the tray of food on Scarlett's bed.

Scarlett scarfed down the eggs and bacon. Even though she'd had a good dinner the night before, the days in the cell had taken their toll on her. What if they were the last few days of her life? What a miserable way to go.

But she wasn't going down without a fight. Now that she was clean and adequately full, she felt more capable. She might not be fully fae, but she was smart and resourceful and would give the looming battle everything she had.

Abigail helped Scarlett dress. For the battle, Scarlett would wear black leather pants and boots, and a leather vest that crossed in front. At least she'd be able to move quickly. Abigail braided Scarlett's hair into two long braids.

"My mother used to braid my hair," Scarlett told Abigail. Speaking of her mother pulled at her chest, but it didn't hurt like it used to—her words felt right.

"Mine, too." Abigail smiled.

What brought Abigail to Faerie? Scarlett had never thought to ask until now. "Why are you here?"

"I don't actually remember," Abigail said. "All I know is I bargained away ten years for part of my memory to be erased."

What happened that was so bad it was worth ten years of servitude? Scarlett changed the subject to a more pleasant topic.

After Scarlett was ready, Abigail left her to go help prepare the food being served to all the guests, giving Scarlett a moment to herself.

Scarlett sat in a chair next to the window overlooking the courtyard, which was filled with fae—all there to witness Summer Court history. To Scarlett, this battle was a fight for her life—for a chance to go home. But to everyone there, it was part of their society. A ritual important to their future.

A knock on the door startled Scarlett. Raith must be back to take her downstairs. When she opened the door, she was surprised to see the Unseelie King staring at her, a smirk on his face. "Don't you look feisty."

"Can I help you?" Scarlett didn't have time for any more games. She couldn't help him pass the time answering all his stupid questions like during The Hunt.

Today, she'd be a participant in the main event. Had he come to cheer her on or watch her fail?

"Meow." Kaelem laughed. "Can I come in for the quickest of moments?"

Scarlett considered telling him no, but he'd been the one to warn her about the feeding ritual, so she should hear him out. She moved from the doorway, letting Kaelem pass. He shut the door with his magic.

"A human in the middle of a Summer Battle of Heirs," Kaelem said. "Life is full of surprises."

"These may be my last moments breathing, so if you have a point, make it." Scarlett didn't mean to be so sharp, but nerves were settling in her stomach and she'd rather be angry than scared.

Kaelem pulled something out of his pocket and held it up—it was a small, silver pill. "I brought you a gift."

"Poison?"

Kaelem laughed. "No, darling. This is a special Unseelie concoction. Take it and you'll have a better chance of winning."

"What is it?"

"Now what fun would telling you be? All you need to know is it will help you, but, with magic, there are always consequences."

Scarlett took the pill from him. What would it do to her? She didn't think help from Kaelem would be worth the cost.

"Thank you," Scarlett said. "But I'll take my chances." She slipped it in her pocket.

"If you insist," Kaelem said.

"Why bother helping me?" Scarlett asked.

"I have my reasons." He shrugged. "Good luck, or as you humans say, break a leg," Kaelem added before disappearing. Apparently, he had no issue evanescing.

A few minutes later, Raith was at her door. Then they were walking to the courtyard. When the crowd saw them, they all cheered. Being chosen as Raith's second, even as a human, must have taken her a step up in class, because no one in the crowd scowled at her.

She and Raith took their spots on the opposite side of the announcer as Cade and Poppy. Scarlett didn't look at either of them. Any nice feelings Scarlett had for Cade vanished the moment she was thrown into the dungeon like some criminal. She'd foolishly thought better of him. Even if she'd always known he was using her, they'd shared moments together that made her believe he had good intentions. But clearly she'd been wrong. He was selfish and would do whatever he needed to do to win the battle against his battle, no matter who he had to hurt in the process.

"You will each be evanesced somewhere random in the forest." The announcer paused and looked at all four of them. "When a brother has won, he can evanesce himself and his second out."

Scarlett wouldn't go in with Raith? She'd be put somewhere else. What if Cade or Poppy found her first? She'd stand no chance against even one of them by herself. She ran her fingers over the pill in her pocket. It would help her, though she didn't know how exactly. Or what the cost would be.

The announcer continued, "You will not be alone. Forest creatures can come and go as they please. The winner will be declared when either Raith or Cade is killed or surrenders."

Scarlett glanced into the crowd and saw Jaser giving her a thumbs up. The announcer counted down from three. She held Jaser's gaze as long as she could, trying to remember everything he'd taught her. The moment the announcer said "one," Scarlett felt herself flying through the air. She landed inside a crumbling castle exposed to the light above. Overgrown branches slithered into the stone walls.

Scarlett exited the collapsing building into the middle of the forest. The staff she'd selected as her weapon choice leaned against a large tree. Not only was she at a disadvantage by being mainly human, but she didn't know the forest like the others did.

Scarlett grabbed the staff. The orb in the middle glowed violet. She could do this. Cade and Poppy wouldn't see her as a threat, so all she needed to do was survive until Raith or Cade won. Then she'd figure out her plan after that.

Raith was somewhere, hopefully not too far away. She didn't know which way to find him, but when she closed her eyes, she could feel him though the bond. He was to her right somewhere.

Scarlett jogged toward the bond. A tree branch shot through the air toward her. She lunged out of its path. The roots rose from the ground and slithered toward her. Raith warned her about this. The forest would play with her mind. This wasn't real. The roots moved swiftly. Scarlett jumped over them. A tree branch swung down. She ducked.

She closed her eyes and inhaled deeply. When she opened them, the tree was back to normal. Scarlett pushed herself from the ground and kept running toward the pull of the bond.

CADE FELT the pull of the bond with Poppy. He sprinted toward it until they nearly ran into each other.

"Found you," Cade said.

"Obviously." Poppy put her hand on her hip. "What's the plan?"

"Let's split up. The sooner we can find Raith and kill him, the sooner we can be done with this."

"What about Scarlett?"

"We'll deal with her when the time comes. She's of no real threat."

"If she gets in the way?"

Cade paused. "Do what you must."

He didn't like the idea of killing a human. Scarlett hadn't asked to be tangled in this web of the Summer Court. Cade had brought her into it all. But it was what it was, and he wouldn't let his sympathy stop him from winning the battle. He was so close. If he killed her, it would be for the better good of his people.

Cade jogged back the direction he came from and Poppy headed straight into the forest. Something growled at Cade from behind a tree, but when Cade snarled, the creature shut up.

Now and again a tree would shift, the forest trying to break into his mind. But with his mental shields so strong, it couldn't get through. Something rustled behind a tree.

He could feel her fear.

"There's no point hiding, I know you're there."

Scarlett stepped out from the cover of the tree trunk with a staff raised in front of her. Her expression was cold as her eyes glared at him.

"It doesn't have to be like this," Cade said. "I don't want to hurt you."

"No, you just want to kill Raith," Scarlett said.

"It must be done."

Scarlett hovered close to the tree. "And I'm what, collateral damage?"

"I never said that."

"You didn't have to. You had me thrown into the fucking dungeon." Scarlett's tone was full of venom. The emotion she exuded made her stronger than she'd been since he'd found her in the cemetery. The pain remained, but it was hidden behind her rage.

"I just needed to stay focused," Cade said. His mother knew that Scarlett had gotten under his skin. Cade needed some distance so he could concentrate on preparing for the battle. "After the battle, I can be myself again. I can protect you."

"It doesn't work like that. You can't blame this on the battle. Whatever you're willing to do to become ruler is who you'll be as king. There's no difference."

That wasn't true. He would do what he needed to do to win and then he could be the king the Summer Court needed.

The orb in the middle of Scarlett's staff caught Cade's attention. It shined purple. But that wasn't possible. It would only glow if the wielder were fae.

Or part fae.

No. It couldn't be. Scarlett glanced at the glowing orb and back to Cade.

"What did Raith do to you?" Cade asked. He'd heard of ways for human to become fae, but they were complicated, dangerous, and dark.

"Raith did nothing," Scarlett snapped. "Except treat me like an equal, unlike you. You knew I was weak. I was just a fox in your trap."

Fury bubbled inside Cade. "Was I so bad for wanting to help some petty human escape her mortal worries? I brought you to a castle. I didn't treat you like a servant."

"Then I got tossed into a cell." Scarlett clenched her jaw.

"How is that glowing?" Cade gestured to the orb.

"I don't really know," Scarlett said. "Things have been different for me ever since I came to Faerie."

Could Cade have missed the fact that Scarlett wasn't entirely human? Her emotion tasted better than any mortal's he'd had before. Was it because she wasn't fully mortal?

If she was part fae, what other powers did she possess? He couldn't risk her getting in the way of him winning this battle. His mother was right. He was too attached. The only way to end it would be to end her.

Cade felt the Summer energy building in his palm. Before he could change his mind, he hurled it at Scarlett.

Her eyes widened as she twirled the staff and hit the magic back at Cade. He wasn't expecting it to fly toward him. As he lunged out of the way, it hit his shoulder, burning a hole through his jacket.

Scarlett's footsteps echoed as he grabbed his wound.

WITH HIS DAGGERS strapped to his back, Raith hurried toward the bond with Scarlett. She couldn't hold her own against either Cade or Poppy, and Raith was the genius who got her into this mess.

Her blood would be on his hands.

He'd never cared to be king, but he'd always had too much pride to just give Cade the crown. But now that his father was actually gone, something in him had changed. He didn't know if Cade would be a good king, not under the influence of Kassandra. Throwing Scarlett into the dungeon had the queen's name written all over it, and the fact that Cade would just let it happen—well, that said plenty.

An arrow sailed past Raith's head. He tumbled behind the cover of a tree. "Well, I know my younger brother didn't choose a bow and arrow as his weapon."

"Hiding, are you? What kind of potential king hides behind a tree like a coward?"

"A pragmatic one," Raith said. "Where's all this hostility coming from? I thought we were friends."

"You leave your friends to fend for themselves in a bar full of drunk assholes?"

Yeah, Raith knew that decision would come back to bite him. He and Poppy had spent some time together a couple of years ago. She had left her training session in a particularly bad mood and nearly ran Raith over. He suggested they get out of Faerie and have a little fun, and, to his surprise, she agreed.

"I couldn't exactly turn down the Unseelie King's invitation." Raith peeked around the tree. An arrow flew at his face.

"None of it matters now. What matters is I'm obligated to try and kill you. Nothing personal."

Raith pulled his daggers out and stepped out from the cover of the tree. Poppy slung another arrow at him. He blocked it with his dagger.

"I thought you were supposed to be the best in the army. Or do people just say that because they're scared of your daddy?"

Poppy snarled and shot another arrow. It missed Raith's shoulder by less than an inch. Raith glanced at Poppy again. She stood a few feet in front of a large tree. He hid behind another tree and closed his eyes, inhaling the energy of the forest around him. He pictured the tree branches swooping down and pulling Poppy into the tree trunk.

"What in the hell?" Poppy yelled.

Raith stepped from behind the tree and toward Poppy. "Don't bother fighting it. It isn't the forest's mind magic."

"How'd you do this?" She struggled but didn't budge.

"My little secret." Poppy's bow had fallen to the ground next to her. Raith picked it up. "Guess you'll have to kill me another time."

"Don't leave me like this," Poppy yelled.

Raith ignored her. He blew her a kiss and sprinted away until he found Scarlett hidden up in a tree.

"Finally," she said as she hopped down. "Cade might be close. I ran into him earlier and sent one of those energy balls back at him."

"I'm sorry I got you into all of this."

And he meant it. He never thought that much about the fragility of human life until now. Or that he'd actually care about the treatment of a human. The anger that radiated through him when he heard they locked Scarlett up had surprised him.

"My older brother apologizing to a human?" Cade stepped into the clearing. "Never thought I'd see the day."

"I always knew you were a momma's boy, but I didn't think you were completely whipped." Raith stood in front of Scarlett and whispered. "Go hide. I can handle my little brother."

"No," Scarlett said. "I'm part of this, too, whether I like it or not."

Raith sauntered toward Cade with his daggers raised; Scarlett stayed a few feet behind him. Cade held his sword in front of him, pointed at Raith's chest. Raith made the first move. He lunged at Cade, swooping his daggers through the air, which were met with the cling of Cade's sword. The two swapped swing for swing, always blocked by the other. Raith needed to get under his brother's skin.

"Even human girls like me better than they like you," Raith said.

Cade swung his sword at Raith's heart. Raith's daggers crossed and blocked it.

"Ah, but Scarlett's not totally human," Cade said. "She's a mutt of some sort."

"Such hostility in your words, brother." Raith sauntered around Cade. "But I'm glad to know any feelings you had for her are long gone. It won't bother you that I slept with her, then."

Rage boomed from Cade. Normally high fae kept their emotions to themselves, so for Raith to feel Cade's anger so strongly must mean he let his shields down. Good.

If Raith could distract Cade, he could use his nature magic to take him off guard. He just needed to find the right moment.

He waited too long. As Raith considered his next move, a blast of Summer energy shot from Cade's left hand, hitting Raith square in the heart.

Chapter Thirty-One

C ade watched his brother fall to the ground. A gaping hole in Raith's vest burned through to his skin. Raith was knocked out cold, his body limp on the ground. Cade held his sword above Raith.

"Stop." Scarlett ran at Cade with her staff in her hands.

"Leave, Scarlett. This is none of your concern."

He couldn't believe that she would sleep with Raith after she turned him down. Cade was the one who had tried to help her. Raith must have done something to her —erased her memories or manipulated them—to change her feelings toward Cade.

When she reached Cade, she swung her staff at him. He blocked it easily with his sword. She couldn't do anything to hurt him, at least not physically. "You fucked him?"

Scarlett's face dropped. "I... we... got lost in a moment."

Cade's anger resurfaced. "You were supposed to be *mine*."

He wasn't good enough for her but his brother was?

Scarlett's brows narrowed as she clenched her jaw. She twirled her staff above her head and brought it down toward Cade's legs. "I belong to no one."

He jumped over the staff and sliced his sword at Scarlett's head. She blocked it with her staff. His sword pushed against it and shoved Scarlett back. She fell to the ground.

"You don't understand," Cade said. "My people need me. Raith cannot become king."

Scarlett stood. "He'd be a far better king than you ever would."

Without thinking, Cade threw a ball of energy at Scarlett, hitting her in the stomach and sending her flying back into a tree, her body sprawled unnaturally on the forest floor.

He'd killed her.

Cade looked at his brother, still unconscious. He was a high fae. He'd heal, but the blow to his chest had been strong. Cade had never had such strong Summer energy than in that moment. He raised the sword above Raith's chest. Scarlett's words from earlier replayed in his head. *Whatever you're willing to do to become ruler is who you'll be as king. There's no difference.*

Would his first act as king be to kill his own brother? He'd already shed the blood of a mortal, because even if Scarlett had some fae blood in her, she was also human.

Raith had saved Cade from the waves as children. A

life debt that Cade still owed his brother coursed through Cade's veins. If he killed him, he'd betray his honor.

It was almost nighttime. The animals would be out soon. He'd let them finish Raith off—one less kill on his soul—and by not killing Raith himself, his debt would be paid.

Cade walked away from Raith's body, the pulsing of the life debt gone.

He was king now.

Cade followed the bond to find Poppy trapped against a tree. He helped her out as she cursed Raith. When he told her he'd killed both Raith and Scarlett, Poppy shut up, surprise on her face.

She bowed to him.

He hadn't actually killed Raith, but he'd be dead soon enough. No one needed to know the truth. It would be his secret. Cade grabbed Poppy's hand and evanesced them back to the crowd.

The elation on his mother's face was the first thing he saw. She grabbed the sides of her dress and curtsied to her son. The crowd followed, the male fae bowing and females curtsying. He returned a bow to them all.

He would be a good king to his people.

Chapter Thirty-Two

I t was almost dark as Scarlett awoke. Her body ached from head to toe as if she'd been run over by a tank. She could barely move. With night so close, she knew if she didn't get up soon, she'd be eaten by something—or worse. An eerie silence swept through the forest. The banshee's face appeared in her thoughts.

Scarlett remembered the pill Kaelem had given her. She reached into her pocket—it was still there. She hadn't planned to take it. There would be a price to pay. But if she didn't, she'd pay the ultimate price: death.

Maybe dying was the best option. She'd finally be free from her grief. But she'd never see her sister again, never make it to her mother's grave. It could end here. Not like this.

Before she could talk herself out of it, Scarlett tossed the pill into her mouth and chewed. It was fruitier than she expected. Delicious, actually. As she swallowed it, her nerves tingled. Within a minute, she could push herself up. Another minute passed and she felt back to normal. Then she felt different. Stronger. Even her vision seemed sharper.

Scarlett rushed to Raith, who had landed on his back, with his arms sprawled awkwardly at his sides. She could hear his heart beating. Wait, she shouldn't be able to hear someone's heart from this far away.

What had that pill done to her?

She didn't have time to care. The light was almost gone. A howl echoed in the distance. Another howl cried closer this time. Scarlett's pulse quickened. She bent next to Raith and placed her hands over the hole in his chest. His skin was covered in blisters where the energy hit him. He looked bad, so bad. Scarlett had been able to heal small wounds, but this was something else.

A new power flowed through her.

Scarlett closed her eyes and imagined the burn being sucked out of Raith. She felt the pain of the energy hitting him, the searing of his skin. She bit her lip but kept pulling the wound out of him. Her eyes grew heavy. She was almost there. Just a little more.

And then she passed out.

RAITH GASPED as he grabbed for his chest. He remembered Cade's energy hitting him. Remembered the pain as it burned through his flesh. Then, nothing. He was out.

The hole in his skin was gone, though his clothing was still burned. Scarlett's body lay next to his, her eyes closed.

He could hear her heartbeat, otherwise he may have thought her dead. Somehow, she must have healed him. But to heal such a deep wound would require more power than she could possibly have as a part human.

Did Cade think Raith was already dead? No, Cade wasn't stupid. For some reason, he'd left Raith to die instead of finishing the job. Typical Cade. Wouldn't want to get his hands too dirty.

Whatever the reason, Raith wasn't complaining.

Raith could hear the music coming from the castle. Cade had claimed his throne—even though he hadn't killed Raith. No one thought to check?

With the night so close, Raith needed to get him and Scarlett out of the forest. After slinging Scarlett over his shoulder, he used the music as his compass to get close to the castle but instead went to his tree house. There, he got a portal door and thought of Silver Lake as he opened it. Neither of them was safe in Faerie now.

Raith found a park bench to lay Scarlett on. He glamoured them both invisible to the mortal world. He didn't know where to take Scarlett, so all he could do was wait for her to wake.

He recognized this place. It was in this parking lot that he saved a human girl. Raith, thanks to his supernatural hearing, heard her tell the guy she was with to stop—she didn't want to go any further. The guy called her a tease. The girl cried out for help as she struggled. Raith could feel her fear.

He had evanesced to the car, opened the door, yanked

the asshole out, and told the girl to run. Then he showed the jerk what it felt to be defenseless.

Scarlett had been defenseless and he'd brought her into the battle. Guilt plagued him as he watched her lying still, only her chest moving as she breathed in and out.

What made him any better than the asshole human? Raith had taken away Scarlett's choice in a different way.

Yet, she'd saved him. He couldn't undo it, but he was relieved they'd both made it out alive.

Raith had once saved Cade, creating a life debt between brothers. That debt had been paid. He could feel it now gone. But a new one had formed in his place, this time *he* the indebted one.

SCARLETT AWOKE, eyes still closed.

Something new surged through her now. With heightened senses, she absorbed the sounds around her. A heart thumped close by. Further away, a bird chirped. And in the distance, a car honked.

Her eyes snapped open.

There were no cars in Faerie.

"You're awake," Raith said. He sat on the ground next to the bench Scarlett lay on.

She sat up and scooted over, making room for Raith. He joined her on the bench.

"What happened?" Scarlett asked.

"You tell me."

Scarlett remembered Raith getting hit with Cade's

magic. She remembered trying to fight him off and getting blasted. She'd awoken injured, night setting in.

Then she remembered taking the pill. As her body absorbed it, something inside her changed. A new power filled her.

"I healed you." She looked to Raith. He seemed healthy.

"How'd you do it?"

"I'm not quite sure."

Raith just stared at her. She wanted to tell him about the pill she had taken and what it had done to her. But she didn't. She was embarrassed she'd given into the temptation Kaelem had given her, even if they'd be dead otherwise. He'd said there would be a cost. What would it be?

"Let's get you home," Raith said.

They walked to her house, which was empty. She wasn't sure how long she'd been gone. Panic filled her. What if Kassandra had got to Ashleigh? Scarlett released her worry Ashleigh was most likely back at school. The house smelled as if it'd been closed off for a while. Kassandra would think Scarlett was dead, giving her no reason to come after her sister.

Though her house seemed plain by comparison to the Summer Court castle, Scarlett was glad she'd made it home. For a while, she had feared it would never happen.

Raith asked if he could stay the night, which, of course, Scarlett allowed.

Scarlett set a blanket and pillow on the couch. "Will this do?"

"Yes," Raith said. "I'm sorry I brought you into this mess."

Scarlett shrugged. "I made it home. That's what matters."

"I shouldn't have told Cade about our night together. Not like that."

No, he shouldn't have. But the anger on Cade's face had sent a chill of satisfaction through Scarlett. She wasn't his pet. Her choices were hers to make, and knowing she'd hurt him by making love to Raith made her happier than she'd have admitted to anyone. Even Raith.

"Good night," Scarlett said.

"Night."

Raith passed out on the couch while Scarlett curled into her mom's bed. Even with her heightened senses, the scent of her mom was long gone now, but the comfort of her room remained.

She could sense Raith, even through the house walls. His emotions ran low, but she could feel dull hatred.

She could still feel the bond.

When Scarlett woke the next morning, Raith was gone. He'd left a note saying they'd meet again, but she had no idea where he'd gone. Part of her felt betrayed— how could he just leave her? But it was better that way. She needed some time to herself.

The weekend came and, as Scarlett had hoped, Ashleigh came back to the house.

"Scarlett!" Ashleigh ran to her sister and pulled her into a hug. "You're alive!"

Scarlett squeezed Ashleigh's waist. She could feel the

relief oozing from Ashleigh. Something was different with Scarlett, but she didn't have time to worry about that at that moment.

"I just needed some time away," Scarlett said. "But I'm back."

Ashleigh didn't press any further. Scarlett asked her how everything had been while she'd been gone, which had apparently been a week and a half. It had been a lot longer in Faerie, but, thankfully, less time had passed here in the mortal world.

The world had carried on without Scarlett—mostly unchanged.

But Scarlett—she was forever altered. Every day she felt a little more different than she had the day before. Her vision continued to improve and her magic felt more innate than it had before. It seemed the effects of the pill from Kaelem weren't immediate. Her transition still continued.

"Wanna go grab a latte with me?" Ashleigh asked the next morning.

"Sure, let me get dressed."

Scarlett picked out jeans and a t-shirt, much different than the dresses she'd worn in Faerie. Scarlett dabbed on some makeup in front of the mirror in her room. She needed much less now that things had *changed*. Her skin radiated a natural vibrancy. Bags no longer lingered under her eyes. Her cheeks constantly blushed pink.

She tucked her hair behind her ears, the tops of which now met in a point.

Chapter Thirty-Three

A s Raith wandered Silver Lake aimlessly, unsure of what to do next, he heard a familiar voice.

"A Summer Prince in the mortal world," Kaelem said behind Raith. "The new Summer King didn't kill you after all."

"Nope." Raith turned to see Kaelem in human clothes, unglamoured. "Surprise, surprise."

Kaelem cocked his head. "I can't say it really surprises me."

Raith shrugged. "What do you want, Kaelem?"

"Can't an old friend be concerned?"

Raith's eyebrow rose. "I didn't know you were capable of concern."

"You're probably right. But I do love drama in the other courts."

"You love drama. Period." The whole reason Kaelem had invited Raith to his court had been to see if he'd ditch

Poppy. Life was a game to Kaelem. Raith knew better than to trust him.

"I like to know things," Kaelem said. "And I know quite a bit about your lovely Summer Court."

"It's not my court anymore." It really wasn't. Even if Cade would welcome him back, which Raith doubted, he didn't want any part of that place. He finally realized he'd never find happiness there.

Kaelem smirked. "Ahh… but I know things about your mother."

CADE SPENT his first night as king of the Summer Court among his people and the guests from the other courts. He was congratulated by the Seelie advisor to the queen, a Spring Court Princess, and the King of the Unseelie Court. The other courts would likely send their best wishes with a gift soon, as was customary when a new ruler took his place.

After the festivities, Cade went to his room alone. He could have bed nearly any female there—except Poppy, she wouldn't do anything she didn't want to do, even for a king—but he wasn't in the mood for sex.

He'd killed Scarlett. For what, jealousy? That wasn't the type of person, let alone king, Cade wanted to be. But he'd spared his brother, sort of. Both Raith and Scarlett would be in the stomach of a cyclops or drained by a banshee by now. But he didn't slice his sword into Raith's chest—his first act of mercy.

The next morning, his mother joined him for breakfast. She was no longer the reigning queen of the Summer Court, but she was still royal, so she wore a smaller crown.

"My son," she said as she sat on the end of the table opposite Cade. "We have many plans to make now."

Plans? Cade had barely been crowned king and the court had no pressing needs that he knew of.

Kassandra continued. "As you know, many years ago, the Seelie and Unseelie Courts moved to the mortal realm and trapped our courts here and bound our abilities, while they are as powerful as they've ever been. It's time we end the curse they've placed upon us."

Sure, there was some hostility when that had happened, but since then, season courts had thrived, even without their full power.

"The Seelie and Unseelie Courts are too powerful," Cade said.

"They won't be if we bind *their* powers."

✿❧✿

SCARLETT STOOD on the familiar hill overlooking the cemetery below. It seemed like forever since she'd been here. Any hint of breeze had abandoned the empty graveyard.

It was better that way—a moment for her and her mom, alone.

The hot summer sun hovered above, its rays shining down on Scarlett and warming her like an embrace. Her feet pushed forward, down the hill and through the graveyard. Scarlett twirled the rose, yellow and beautiful, in her hand. She'd picked it from her mom's garden that morning.

When she arrived at her mom's grave, her chest tightened.

Scarlett inhaled deeply as she stared at her mother's name engraved on the headstone. So much had changed since she'd last been here—the same day Cade had found her. Instead of facing her fears, she'd run like a coward. But she'd learned she was stronger than she'd ever known. Her mother had raised her well.

Scarlett breathed in the grief that struck her. Not only did she miss her mother with her entire being, but if anyone would have believed Scarlett's story, it would have been her.

Unlike Scarlett, who never *listened* to her mom, not when she was having a fit. But now, after Scarlett had seen so much, she couldn't help but wonder if her mother's illness was more than anyone thought.

If Scarlett had the gifts she had now, could she have healed her mother? It was unlikely, but she could have at least tried.

Tears dripped down her cheeks. What-ifs were pointless. Scarlett couldn't let her heartache consume her any longer.

Scarlett placed the rose in front of the stone and walked away.

Whims of Fae

About the Author

Nissa Leder was born and raised in Washington State, but now lives in the sunny Phoenix Valley with her husband, Joe, and their two boxers, two cats, and pet poison dart frogs.

Always an avid reader, she didn't realize her love for writing her own stories until her freshman year in college. Once she knew her life's calling, she began studying the craft of writing and eventually obtained an MFA from Spalding University.

When she isn't writing down the stories that fill her head, she's likely at the tennis courts working on her forehand or journeying to another world by reading a book. She's a big believer in following your dreams and encourages everyone to shoot for the moon and pursue their passions.

 facebook.com/nissa.leder

 twitter.com/nissaleder

instagram.com/nissaleder

27026126R00162

Made in the USA
Columbia, SC
25 September 2018